Five reasons why you'll love this book

A new and original world to explore—
including the smells!

✦⟨⊗⟩✦

An unlikely hero who you'll be
rooting for all the way.

✦⟨⊗⟩✦

A whole cast of brilliantly
despicable baddies.

✦⟨⊗⟩✦

Discover that being different is what
makes each one of us special.

✦⟨⊗⟩✦

A talented new author who writes with
an exciting and unique voice.

To my parents, for filling our
house with books and love.

OXFORD
UNIVERSITY PRESS

Great Clarendon Street, Oxford OX2 6DP
Oxford University Press is a department of the University of Oxford.
It furthers the University's objective of excellence in research, scholarship,
and education by publishing worldwide. Oxford is a registered trade mark
of Oxford University Press in the UK and in certain other countries

First published 2017

British Library Cataloguing in Publication Data

Data available

ISBN: 978-0-19-274582-8

1 3 5 7 9 10 8 6 4 2

Printed in Great Britain

Paper used in the production of this book is a natural,
recyclable product made from wood grown in sustainable forests.
The manufacturing process conforms to the environmental
regulations of the country of origin.

MOLD AND THE POISON PLOT

LORRAINE GREGORY

OXFORD
UNIVERSITY PRESS

Chapter 1

When I was a wee babe no bigger an a marrow, Mam put me in the dustbin an left me out fer the binmen.

But the binmen didn't want me neither.

Wouldn't have made any money from me, see. They do make a pretty penny fer babies at the rag market but people mostly want fair an bonny ones an I was small an scraggy as a drowned rat with a massive great hooter to boot. That's what old Aggy says anyway. She's the one what found me at the dump an lucky fer me she took me home an raised me up. Lucky fer her too cos who else'd put up with all her moanin?

'Mold!' she bellows at me from the cellar. 'Run down Grevel's Ginhouse and fetch me a nip of something fore I catch me death of cold!'

'An what am I supposed to pay Grevel with?' I yell back. 'You ain't paid the old skinflint fer last week's grog yet, he aint gonna give me any more.'

She drinks too much fer my likin. The reek of it oozes

from her pores an spite the lavender she tucks in her clothes to try an disguise it I can smell the sourness a mile off. She says it keeps her warm an eases the ache in her bones but she'll be drinkin away the rent soon if I let her. Our ramshackle old cottage might be damp an drafty with a roof more rot than thatch but it's all we got tween us an the gutter.

'He will if ye ask nice!' Aggy insists.

'No, he flamin well won't. He'll tell me to get lost an kick me out fer good measure.' I can almost feel the bruise on me backside from the last time an I aint goin back fer the same again I can tell ye that much. 'Anyway, I said I'd go an visit Begsy tonight.'

'Begsy? Lawks Mold, why'd you wanna spend all your time with that crusty old one-legged sailor?'

'Cos, he's me mate. An I like his stories.' I inch me way towards the door, hopin I can get out fore she kicks up a stink.

'Yeah well, you just remember they're only stories. Don't you be getting any funny ideas about running off to sea!'

'Course I won't you daft bat!' I open the door real quiet an look out at the filth-lined alleyways. 'How could I leave all this behind?' I mutter.

'And you get back here before dark Mold, y'hear me? If you're caught out after curfew they're liable to give you a flogging!'

'I know, don't worry,' I shout an then I'm out the door an runnin. I pelt down Ekle Street, ignorin the stench from the open sewer that runs down the alley an the snot-nosed kids grubbin fer scraps in the trash.

I bang on Begsy's front door an he hollers at me to come in. He's sittin in his ratty old armchair by the fire puffin on his pipe an fillin the front room with a pungent sweet smoke. Under it there's the faint whiff of hot meat pie that makes me mouth water but I don't say nothin cos I never did like askin Begsy fer handouts.

'All right lad?'

'Aye, an you?'

'Not so bad, my leg's giving me gyp as usual but no point complaining is there?' He lets out a sigh an adjusts the carved wooden peg that fits on his stump. He's worn it from before I was even born, ever since Boggers sunk his ship in the harbour an he gashed his leg on a rock. Gangrene got in an they had to cut it off below the knee fore it killed him.

'Want me to chop ye some more wood? Yer nearly out.'

'Ah, that'd be grand lad.'

I kneel down on the floor an take the chopper to the logs he's got lined up by the fireplace. The cold makes his leg worse so he needs a good supply.

'There's some leftover pie on the table, why don't you have a slice? All that hard work's bound to make you hungry.' Me belly rumbles loudly in reply an Begsy laughs. 'Go on lad, have it now before you start chewing on the furniture.'

I finish stackin the pile of chopped wood, give Begsy a quick grin an rush over to the table where a thick slab of meat an potato pie in golden pastry sits waitin fer me. I cut a smallish piece an fork the gravy-covered fillin into me mouth, tryin not to groan out loud. There was only bread an drippin fer tea tonight an it barely touched the sides.

'That's a proper nice pie Begsy. Did ye get if from Meg?'

'Aye, she's got a good touch with the pastry hasn't she? Go on, have a bigger bit. A growing lad like you needs to keep your strength up.'

I shouldn't really but I can't help it. I scoff down another slice an finally the clawin hunger starts to fade.

'Blimey Mold, you're sprouting like a weed! Those trews are too short already.'

'I know.' I look a proper pillock an all cos the ragged ends don't even reach me ankles but we aint got the money fer new ones. Not since they upped the flamin taxes again.

'Seems like only yesterday Aggy brought you home in nappies and now look at you.' Begsy shakes his head, his eyes all misty like they get when he's lost in a memory. I reckon it's too good a chance to miss.

'D'you remember it well then?'

'Aye, I'll never forget it. It's not every day your friend

brings a baby home from the dump is it?'

'Was I wrapped in a blanket when she brung me home? Was there a letter tucked inside? Anythin at all about where I come from?'

Begsy gets up an taps his pipe out in the fire. 'Why the sudden interest in all this, Mold?'

'I dunno. I saw Matty Hargreaves an her new baby the other week an it made me wonder that's all.'

'Wonder what?'

'If my ma ever loved me like that.'

Begsy sighs an rubs his face. 'I'm sorry Mold. You need to be asking Aggy not me.'

'I did ask her! I asked her an asked her but she won't tell me nothin.'

'Then that's up to her.' His voice is firm but his eyes won't meet mine. I reckon he knows sommink but he won't tell me, not if Aggy's asked him not to. 'So, any news from the market today?'

'Nah.' I huff out a breath.

'Must be something.' Begsy nudges me an passes me a mug of tea from the pot. I have a sip.

'Well, there was some gossip about the Boggers bein cannibals.'

'What?'

'Tucker said it. He reckons the Boggers ate people durin the war. Cooked em up in a big pot an everythin.'

Begsy tuts an raises his eyes to the heavens. 'Tucker

Parks talks out of his backside. The Boggers didn't eat anyone. They killed people sure enough but they weren't cannibals.'

'Oh.' I thought it was probably a lie but you never know do ye? Them Boggers had done some pretty bad things durin the war.

'And why are you hanging around with Tucker anyway?' Begsy demands. 'That boy's nothing but trouble.'

'I wasn't hangin round with him, I just saw him down the market,' I explain fore he can go off on one. 'Ma Hibbert said someone had seen a Bogger in Westenburg an Tucker said they was all gonna come an eat us. That's all.'

'Boggers in Westenburg? Pah, those rumours surface every so often, Mold, but that's all they are. King Godric spent years killing them off, there's nothing but snakes and lizards in that swamp now.'

'That's what I told him.'

'And he didn't give you any bother then?' Begsy asks, peerin at me fer signs of bruises.

'Nah. I told ye, ever since I blacked both his eyes he's been nice as pie.'

'Just as well for him.' Begsy relaxes back in his chair. 'Now, I've got a good tale for you if you like?'

'Is it about cannibals?' I ask.

'No. Now just you sit and listen and you might learn something.'

I sit down on the rug by his feet, enjoyin the full feelin

in me belly, the heat from the fire, an the sound of Begsy's voice in me ear.

⁂

It's near dusk when I leave Begsy's house an grey clouds are spittin drizzly rain down on the alleyways. I'm loaded up with the rest of the pie an half a jar of grog he insisted I have cos he knows what Aggy's like when she aint got none. I step careful like over the rat-infested piles of rubbish an keep an ear cocked fer trouble. The Dregs aint the place to be runnin round in after dark an I'm keen to get back home.

There's a scufflin behind me. I spin round but I can't see anyone. I can smell em though. The sour stink of pickled eggs sends a shudder ripplin down me spine an I duck down the next alley quicker an a fox down a rabbit hole.

Half a second later Ramsey Bendall, night watchman, pickled egg muncher, an general toerag mooches past, stuffin a handful of silver sovs in his purse. I'd bet anythin ye like he's never come by em honest.

'Has the old goat gone yet?' The sudden whisper makes me near jump out me skin till I spot the one yellow eye glowin up at me from somewhere near me knees.

'Aye, he's gone.'

'Thank the stars for that. All this hiding makes a fellow fair thirsty you know . . .' Crippled Bill gazes longingly at the grog I'm carryin.

I sigh an pass him the jar. 'Just a nip mind you.' I yank it back out of his filthy hands fore he can drain it dry. 'Now let me get home will ye.'

'Aye, you better hurry back if you don't want to miss your visitor.'

'What?'

He sniffs an waves his hand over at my door. 'A visitor, some fancy toff, he's round at your house now.'

'Toff? What toff?' I'm talkin to the back of his head though. Crippled Bill's wheelin himself away in the old wooden cart he uses fer legs, off to plague someone else no doubt.

He must be imaginin things . . . what would a toff be doin at my house? I hurry back all the same just to check an I'm about to pull the handle when the door flies open an near smacks me in the face. A whip-thin man in a dark cloak rushes out, bargin straight into me. There's a rancid, sour stink clingin to his skin like a sickness an it sets me teeth on edge.

'Careful mister!' I snap cos he near made me drop the grog.

He turns round an stares at me like I'm sommink a dog sicked up. 'Make way for your betters, guttersnipe.'

'If I see any I will.' I say but I do it quiet like cos there's sommink menacin in his eyes.

'What did you say?' He leans in towards me, I can't stop starin at the black clover mark that's been tattooed high up on his cheek.

'Nothin,' I mumble, steppin away from him an his sour stink.

'Thought so.' He sniffs, tucks sommink in his pocket, an stomps off in his black snakeskin boots. I stick me tongue out at his back an head inside.

'What was that stuck-up toff doin here?' I yell down the stairs after dumpin everythin on the old pine table an shakin the rain off.

'Did ye get me any grog?'

'Begsy gave me a pie. Come up an have sommink to eat.'

'I aint hungry. I'm thirsty.'

'Well, he gave me some grog an all,' I admit.

'I'll be up now.' There's a clatter an some groanin an then she heaves herself up the stairs an stomps over to the table in a flounce of musty skirts an shawls. She pours a mug of grog an downs it in a gulp. Belches. Sits down an pours another mug. 'Ah, now that's better.'

'Right, you've had yer grog—now tell me who that tattooed toff was an what he was doin here?'

'Oh stop fussing Mold! Everything's fine, it's dandy in fact so just sit down and eat yer pie.' Her face is pasty an fleshy an her eyes are squished in like the currants in a bun but when she smiles I can't help but love her.

'You sure?'

'Yes!'

I get outta couple of plates an cut two pieces of pie, pushin one in Aggy's direction.

'Who was he then?' I ask again, determined to find out what was goin on. Aggy rolls her eyes but I can tell she aint cross really.

'A customer, that's all. He come special to see me, said I was the only one who could help so I gave him what he wanted an look. . .' She fishes sommink out of her apron pocket an opens her hand to let me see.

'A parvel?' I stare at the thick gold coin snuggled in her fat palm. 'He gave you a parvel?'

'He did.' Aggy tucks the coin away again as if it might disappear or sommink.

'What did he want fer that?' I ask. I aint ever even seen a parvel more an once or twice. A parvel was enough to feed us fer a month.

'Nothin you need to worry about,' she insists. But I do cos it sounded like trouble to me an trouble was sommink I liked to avoid.

'I don't like it,' I mutter. 'He didn't smell right to me an you're always sayin I should trust me nose.'

'Well, maybe you should trust old Aggy this time.' She reaches over an rubs me head. 'I know what I'm doing pet and if this carries on we'll be eating pies for our supper every bleeding day!'

I watch her sittin there, chucklin an swiggin her grog an hope that fer once in her life she's actually right.

Next mornin me an Aggy go down the rag market, I set her up at our stall with her wicker baskets of potions an head off into the crowds.

It's my job to find the customers see, has been since I was a nipper cos me nose aint like no one else's. I can use it to sniff out people that need help, if they're sick or in pain or afraid or whatever I can tell from the pong they give off so I send em round to see Aggy an she fixes em up.

Aggy reckons it's a gift what I can do but I aint so sure havin a nose twice the size of anyone else's should be called a blessin.

Course, most of the toffs come down the rag market just cos they reckon it's fun to mix with the poor folk. They like to gawk at all the cripples an freaks like me, then get their palms read an head back home with a story to tell.

But every now an then there's a toff I stay well away from no matter what. One who makes me guts roil with the putrid stink that surrounds em an I know straight off that whatever ails em can't be fixed cos it's deep inside em like a canker eatin at their hearts.

That same rancid pong oozed out of that tattooed toff last night. Whatever Aggy says I don't trust him. I keep me eye out fer him all day hopin he might turn up an I can find out just what his game is but all I see are ladies in fancy frocks that wanna buy rosehips for their lips an chalk for their faces.

When the last of the customers are gone I head back to help Aggy pack up, hopin some of the toffs I'd sent her way had parted with their sovs an there'd be enough fer a decent nosh up tonight. As I get closer I can hear someone hollerin up a storm an I wonder who's started kickin off now. It's only when I get round the corner that I realize it's my Aggy makin all the noise. Two city guards are draggin her away from the stall while she yells an fights like a cornered cat.

I run over to try an stop em but a fat, sweaty-faced guard gets in me way.

'Lemmego!' I struggle in his grip. 'What are you doin with her?'

'What's it to you, nosy?' the guard asks with half a snigger. 'That's a good one aint it? Nosy? Cos your nose is so big?'

'Why are you takin her? What's she done?'

'This here's city business boy, nothing to do with you.'

'But she's me family!'

'Family? You an her? Pull the other one lad.'

'She is!' I insist, pullin away from him at last.

'Nah, don't reckon so. Your family must be them ephalumps in the zoo, your nose is about the same size!' He chortles at his own joke.

'Well you must be related to the pigs in the sty over there cos you smell just like em!'

'You cheeky bleeder!' The guard charges at me, fists

raised but his mate steps in an pulls him away, sends him over to see to the horses. Perhaps he can tell from the restless mutterin in the crowds that it won't take much to push em over the edge.

'Look,' he says to me, his voice hushed. 'We're under orders to arrest old Aggy and take her to Westenburg.'

'Arrest her? What for?'

'For murder lad, that's what.'

'Nah, you've made a mistake,' I tell him. 'Aggy aint murdered no one!'

'Well, the orders come from Lord Nash himself to lock her up for poisoning the King so that's what we're doing.'

'Ye mean the King's dead?'

'No.' He sniffs an wipes his nose on his sleeve. 'Not yet anyway but likely he will be soon an then she'll have to pay for what she done.'

I can't believe it. Poisonin the King? They were mad. They must be.

I watch the guards shove Aggy into their wagon an slam the doors shut. Her chubby, tear-stained face peers through the bars an finds me standin there.

'It aint true Mold! I swear it aint true.'

I wait there an watch while the horses drag her away. All I can think of is that ruddy parvel sittin in her hand an wonder exactly what that toff had bought with it.

Chapter 2

I run straight home an slam the door behind me, wishin I could shut out the memory of Aggy bein dragged away just as easy. It's no good though. Every time I close me eyes I can see her face behind those bars.

She's really gone an done it this time. Poisonin the King's a hangin offence fer sure an with her record they won't bother with a trial at all. Just string her up till her neck cracks an let the crows feast on her eyeballs . . .

The eel pasty I had fer tea leaps into me throat an I retch over the slop pail, emptyin me belly over an over till there's nothin left but green, sour bile.

Damn an blast her, why didn't she listen to me? I've told her a hundred times not to touch a flamin poison again. An after she nearly got pinched last year she promised me she wouldn't. Crossed her heart an everythin.

I get up from the floor an rinse me mouth out with water. I know in me bones Aggy'd never do nothin to hurt the King. She loves Godric. Thinks the sun shines out of his backside cos he defeated the Boggers that killed her whole family durin the war. She won't even listen when people blame him fer all the trouble in the Dregs. That stinkin toff must have tricked her somehow, it's the only answer.

There's a sudden loud clatterin at the door, like fists are poundin on the wood.

'Get lost!' I yell, me voice catchin in me throat. It's probly just the gossips comin round to try an weedle out what's happened. It don't take five minutes fer bad news to spread round here.

The poundin stops. Silence creeps into the room remindin me that I'm all alone now. Without Aggy fer the first time in me life. Me legs start tremblin an go all wobbly. I slump down at the table but knowin Aggy won't never sit down here next to me again makes me eyes sting.

I can't believe she'd do this to me. To us.

I swipe at the wet patches on me face. I need to find proof, I need to know if she'd broke her word or not an there's only one way to do that. I grab a candle an head down the worn stone steps to the cellar fore I can change me mind.

The pong sets me coughin soon as I push through the heavy wool curtain that covers the entrance. Great sheaves of dried herbs line the rafters an the shelves are stuffed with pot after pot of stinkin goo. On the straw-lined floor there are rows of old boots growin mushrooms an toadstools and an old iron bath filled with frogs an newts an waterplants.

I wanna smash it up. Break all her precious jars an bottles. Stamp on all her rotten ingredients an grind em into dust so she can never make another flamin poison again but now I'm down here the memories are floodin back.

In the far corner there's a long oak table with pestle, mortar, knives, an spoons. I spent me first years under that table, playin round Aggy's feet as she ground up her wares an made her potions but the bigger I got the worse I found it. All the different smells fogged up me head an made it throb. Made me cough an sputter like a dyin horse.

I thought Aggy'd be cross with me but she just smiled an pinched me cheeks an told me to stay upstairs, so I did. I aint set foot in the cellar fer years. I'd forgotten how cold it is, how damp. I picture Aggy down here all alone, bones achin, strugglin to find the money to pay the rent each week an buy food an clothes . . .

Shame sticks like a stone in me throat. It don't matter whether she made the flamin poison or not, Aggy's all I got in the world. How can I blame her fer tryin to make a bit extra? Me own mam took one look at me an left me in the bin but Aggy raised me an loved me like her own, spite the size of me nose. I owe her. I can't abandon her now, whatever she may have done.

I should go an see Begsy, that's the best thing I reckon.

He'll know what to do, he always does. Feelin happier now I've got a plan I move the heavy curtain outta the way an a great billow of grey smoke smothers me an makes me cough.

The stink of burnin straw fills me nose an I fight me way through it an up the stairs quick as I can. Soon as I see the huge red an golden flames devourin the thatch like hungry monsters I know there's no way to stop it. Nothin I can do to save our house from burnin to the ground.

I might just burn with it if I don't get out.

I can barely see cos the smoke's so thick it makes me eyes smart an sting. I manage to sniff out the faintest hint of fresh air creepin in through the gap round the door though so I drop to me knees an crawl towards it . . .

Nearly . . .

Nearly there . . .

The metal catch burns me hand but I yank down anyway, desperate to escape, only nothin happens. The door won't move. I push harder but there's no give at all. I bang on the wood an yell fer help but the smoke makes me lungs burn an I cough so hard I think I'm gonna be sick.

I turn back round but the fire's everywhere now an I'm frozen like a statue, fear grippin at me heart with icy fingers.

Part of the roof collapses, it misses me by inches an showers me with painful sparks, forcin me to move.

There's no other choice but to head back down the cellar so I crawl across the floor, me hands an knees burnin as I go.

I almost fall down the steps cos it's so hard to see now but the relief of bein out of the smoke an heat, even fer a minute, makes up fer it. I splash some of the water from the bath over me face an dunk me hands in fer relief but there aint enough water to make a dent in the fire, more's the pity.

I watch helplessly as the flames follow me down the steps. I back up till I'm pressed against the wall an that's when I feel a slight draft on me neck an remember. The coal hole!

I leap on to the table in the corner an start bangin on the wooden slats above me. The cellar was supposed to be used fer coal but we'd boarded up the hole the coal man used to drop his wares in years ago. If I could just break the slats I'd be able to climb out an escape bein roasted like a hog on a spit.

The wood's crumblin an rotten an I manage to smash through two of the boards. The blast of fresh air's like balm on me lungs but skinny as I am the gap's still not big enough fer me to get out. I rip at the third board but it's well nailed down an I know I'll never move it on me own.

'Help!' I yell through the gap. 'Help me, please!' I pray someone can hear me over the roarin noise cos the flames are gettin closer. Glass jars are explodin in the heat an the herbs are burnin like billy-oh, makin me even more dizzy.

'Please!' I beg, pullin at the iron nails with me fingertips.

'Hold on lad!' The sound of Begsy's voice almost makes me sob. The last plank is yanked away an he reaches his strong arms down to pull me up into the sweet, fresh air.

Begsy helps me stumble away from the burnin house an lets me collapse on the ground by the old walnut tree where I lie in a heap, coughin fit to burst.

'Thanks,' I manage to rasp out after a few minutes.

'It's a flaming miracle I heard you lad. I was only passing this way so I could fetch some more buckets from Grevel's.'

'I thought I was gonna die in there. You saved me life Begsy.'

He shakes his head. 'I should have come straight in and got you, soon as I saw the fire but he said the house was empty, that you'd already gone.'

'What? Who said that?' I splutter.

'Some tattooed toff standing outside your house.'

Chapter 3

When I finally stop coughin, Begsy helps me up an I stumble round to the front of me house. Everyone's there, a great crowd of Dreggers, standin in a line an throwin buckets of water on the houses next to mine.

'They can't save yours, Mold, but if the rest catch fire the whole place'll go up,' Begsy whispers in me ear. I nod. It's true. The Dregs are like a tinderbox with all the houses made of wood an thatch an built so close together. That's why we're all so careful. Why I can't figure out how the cursed fire had started in the first place.

'Mold!' Meg, the cook from the ginhouse rushes over an wraps me in a blanket. 'Thank heaven you're all right! What happened?'

'I dunno. I was in the cellar an when I come up the house was already burnin. I tried the door but it wouldn't open . . .'

Me eyes dart over to the door lookin fer answers an

through the smoke an flames I can just make out two planks nailed right across it . . . I remember the poundin on the door earlier. I thought it was someone knockin but no . . .

Someone had barred the door.

Barred the door an then set fire to the thatch.

Knowin I was inside.

An then they'd stood outside an told people the house was empty . . .

It all came down to that toff. It must do. Aggy bein arrested, the house burnin, everythin.

Dizziness swamps me an the next thing me legs give way.

'Easy there lad.' Begsy's strong arms catch me an he scoops me up like a babe. 'I'll take him back to mine,' he tells Meg an as he walks away I watch the wooden frame finally give way an me home collapses in a heap behind me.

❧

Mornin seeps through the window an jabs me in the eyes. It takes me a minute to figure out where I am but then I cough an the ache in me chest reminds me exactly what happened last night.

The door opens an Begsy comes in holdin a hot cup of tea. 'Here you go lad, drink this.'

'Thanks.' I take a few sips an it helps soothe me throat.

Begsy sits down on the armchair an looks at me, his face serious.

'Right, I think you need to tell me what's going on. Aggy got carted off for poisoning the King yesterday. The same night your house goes up in flames, some tattooed toff denies you're in there, and you barely get out alive.'

I let out a sigh an tell him what I know.

'Damn and blast,' he growls. 'Aggy's been set up good and proper. This is bad, Mold.'

'I know, that's why I've gotta find that toff, Begsy, find out what he's really up to fore they hang Aggy.' I get off the sofa spite the tremblin in me legs an start searchin fer me clothes.

Begsy shakes his head. 'Men with tattoos like that are bad news Mold. He's probably in some assassins' guild or worse.'

'So what? I aint scared of him or his stupid gang!' I tell him, pullin on me singed trews an tryin to convince meself it's true.

'Well you should be lad! I'd bet my last sov he's been paid to kill the King, set Aggy up to take the blame, and get rid of any witnesses who could say different.'

'I don't care.' I shrug on my tunic even though it's black an stinks of smoke. 'I'm gonna get him for what he's done!'

'Don't be daft lad! You're the key witness!' Begsy snaps. 'He thinks you're dead now and that means you're safe. If he catches sight of you again I doubt you'll be so lucky, so you stay well away from him, you hear me?'

'Aye I suppose yer right . . . but what do I do now? I can't just let Aggy get hanged can I?'

'No,' Begsy huffs out a big breath. 'No, of course you can't. That's why you're going to Westenburg to find out what was in that poison.' He takes a good look at me an frowns.

'What? You want me to go to the city dungeons an ask Aggy what she put in that poison?'

'Aggy never made that poison,' he says, rummagin round in a big wooden chest in the corner.

'Wait. What? How d'you know that?'

'Because she told me. I saw her yesterday morning. She couldn't wait to tell me about the parvel the toff'd paid her for one of her special strengthening tonics. One she'd been famous for making during the war.' He throws a pair of old trews an a ragged tunic at me. 'Put those on. You can't wear those filthy clothes to the city.'

'But . . . why would that toff pay a parvel fer some old tonic? I thought it was cos it was a poison he paid so much?'

'I think he only gave her that because it's going to make her look guilty isn't it? Some old lady from the Dregs with a parvel in her pocket?' I can see he's right straight off an though I'm fumin at the toff fer settin her up so easy I'm real glad Aggy hadn't broke her word.

'All right, but I still don't get it. Why do we need to know what's in this poison?' I slowly undress an pull on the clothes Begsy gave me. They're way too long but at least they don't stink of smoke.

'Because, Mold,' Begsy grabs his shears from the mantel an bends down at me feet. 'The only surefire way to stop them from hanging Aggy is to save the King. The only way to save the King is to find the cure, and the only way we can do that, is if we know exactly what was in that poison.' He finishes hackin the bottoms off me trews an folds up the ends so they're all smart.

'But . . . how'm I supposed to find out what was in some poison the King took yesterday?'

'You'll have to use that amazing nose of yours.' He starts snippin at the sleeves of me tunic.

'Me nose aint amazin ye daft sod. It's just big an horrible.' I slump back down on the sofa.

'Don't be stupid Mold! It's a gift.' Begsy folds up me sleeves an steps back so he can get a good look at his handiwork.

'It aint a flamin gift!' It felt more like a curse to me. It was the reason me ma left me in the bin, it must have been. Aggy said that was rubbish. That there were lots of reasons she might have left me but I couldn't stop thinkin it anyway.

'Come on Mold, I know very well that you can smell almost anything. If you get to the King and sniff his breath I reckon you'll be able to smell whatever was in that poison and if you go and tell Aggy she'll know how to cure it.'

'I might be able to,' I admit, but there are giant butterflies dartin about in me belly at the idea of headin to the city all on my own. Aggy's never let me leave the Dregs before. Let alone go all the way to Westenburg. 'But how'm I supposed to get into the castle to sniff his stupid breath in the first place, clever clogs? Fly into his room usin me fairy wings or sommink?'

Begsy shrugs. 'We'll work it out when we get there.'

'We?'

'Aye.' He raises one eyebrow. 'You don't think I'm gonna let you loose in the city on your own, do you?'

I throw meself at him so hard he stumbles backwards but then he rights himself an his arms go round me an hug me tight.

'We'll get her back, lad,' he whispers in me ear. 'I'd bet my leg on it.'

Chapter 4

Me an Begsy hitch a ride to the city with Ted the barrel man. Aggy saved his daughter from the pox when she was a babbie so he's more an happy to help.

We wedge ourselves in between the cedar wood barrels, a basket of Meg's food on me lap an a worn out blanket spread over us.

Ted flicks his reins at his pair of shires an we start movin. The wagon rumbles an bumps over the rocky track that leads out of the Dregs an away from the only home I've ever known.

Long hours of backside-numbin travellin later Westenburg finally comes into view with the sun settin like a ball of yellow flame behind it. Built right on top of Farley Hill, the city rises up into the sky an then sprawls down the hillside towards the river an the docks.

The wide, sky-blue Verlaw River that cuts right the way through Pellegarno is the only thing separatin us from the Boglands on the other side. I can't help wonderin if any of them rumours I heard are true, if there really are still Boggers livin over there an if they're anything like the enormous green monsters from me nightmares.

The wagon speeds up the main road towards the city stables as our horses, Samson an Delilah, catch a whiff of their oats. It's hard to see much of the city in the evenin light but hundreds of new smells pour into me head like a flood, batterin at me brain till I'm dizzy an me head's fit to burst.

I start coughin an I can't stop. Me chest's sore anyway from all the smoke I breathed in yesterday but now it feels like it's gonna rip apart.

Pretty soon I'm splutterin so hard I can't hardly breathe an then everythin goes black an I crumple onto the wagon bed like a newborn calf.

I can feel Begsy's arms go round me an he pulls me close against him, tucks me in against his side an presses me face hard against his chest, shuttin out the fog of smells. At first it feels like he's smotherin me but then the coughin eases, me head clears, an all I can smell is Begsy.

The scent of soap an tobacco calms me, takes me back to when I was a nipper an Begsy'd come an take me fer a walk. He'd haul me up on his shoulders an we'd stroll along talkin to everyone an I'd pretend like he was me pa.

The deeper I breathe the more one smell takes over all the rest. Mint, honest an strong bursts up from the core of him an washes over me like a wave. It's like the opposite of sniffin out the bad an evil in people. I been doin that for ever, like an instinct almost but this, this was sommink new . . . this was like gettin a glimpse deep inside his heart.

When Begsy lets me go I wait fer the coughin to start again. It don't, thank the stars, but me head's buzzin with all the new pongs.

'You all right, lad?' Begsy asks.

I nod. 'I am now. Cheers.'

'No problem. I reckon all the smells in this place are a bit overwhelming!'

'There's just so many of em . . .'

'Well, you've got a while to get used to them. We'll stay here tonight with the horses, get a few hours' kip and then start our search in the morning.' He gives me a smile, pats me on the shoulder, then goes to help Ted unload the barrels.

Ted heads home soon after an me an Begsy get snuggled in among the straw. I yawn so loud me jaw cracks.

'Goodnight lad.'

'Begsy? Thanks fer comin with me an that, fer helpin me save Aggy.'

'Aye, well Aggy's worth saving. She's helped half the people in the Dregs with something or other. Birthing babies, setting bones, curing fever and she never took a penny from them who couldn't afford it. I'll do what I can to save her, Mold. I promise you that.'

Begsy settles back to sleep but I can't keep quiet. I have to ask.

'What if I can't sniff out the poison though, Begsy? I aint tried nothin like that fore now. What if I can't do it?'

'You will.'

'But if I can't then the King's gonna die an Aggy's gonna hang an it'll all be my fault!' I can't keep the panic from me voice.

'You can do it lad. I know you can.'

'How? How do you know?'

'Listen, I've known you all your life and I've seen what you can do with that nose of yours.' He turns to me in the dark, his eyes lock with mine, belief shinin bright in their depths. 'You were born to do this Mold, trust me.'

'All right.' I let out a breath an try an believe the way Begsy does.

'And if anything did ever happen to Aggy you've always got a home with me my lad. You know that, right?'

I can't speak. Me throat's blocked with all the things I feel but I nod at Begsy an he smiles at me an rubs me head. 'Off to sleep now lad, you'll need a good rest for tomorrow.'

Chapter 5

I wake up when the dawn light creeps through the stable doors, feelin groggy an light-headed from the bad dreams that plagued me. I climb outta the straw anyway an give Begsy a nudge with me foot. He groans an opens his eyes slowly.

'Uuurgh, I'm too old to sleep in a stable, Mold. Much too old.'

'You aint old, Begsy. Just grumpy.' I go an fetch him a dipper of water from the trough an he swigs it down.

'I'm grumpy *because* I'm old.'

I snort an finish off the water. 'You been old all yer life then?'

Begsy mutters sommink under his breath but he gets up out of the hay an heads outside fer a pee. I splash a bit of water on me face an wander over to Meg's basket. I sniff out a leftover pork pie in the corner an tuck in.

Begsy comes back an grabs a boiled egg, peels off the shell with his strong fingers, an munches it down in a couple of bites.

'Thank heaven for Meg, eh Mold?' I smile at him, mouth full of pastry. 'Right then, no time to waste is there? Let's get going.'

I follow Begsy out into Westenburg, the mornin light hurts me eyes fer a minute but then I can't stop gawkin.

The buildins here are big an tall an they're all made out of brick an stone nearly, an the road's cobbled all proper like with no open sewer runnin down the middle. When I ask Begsy he says it all goes underground in pipes.

'Why does it still smell of pee round here then?' I ask him.

'Does it?' He takes a big sniff. 'I can't smell it. I guess it must be from the tannery on the other side of town. They use it there to cure the leather.'

I follow Begsy past hundreds of small, ramshackle houses all crammed in higgeldy piggeldy on either side of the narrow street. There are hundreds of kids playin out in the narrow lanes an it's almost as crowded an noisy as the Dregs.

'I never thought there'd be so many people,' I mutter as we try an squeeze through the crowds.

'It's got much worse since I was here last. There are so many people now they're running out of land to farm. Ted told me that Lord Nash has been buying in grain and food from the other Isles, despite Godric's reluctance. I suppose we should thank the stars there's one royal who gives a stuff for the poor folk.'

When we finally arrive back at the huge wooden gates we come through last night he stops in front of a large well.

'Westenburg is a fortified town, it's built for defence,' Begsy explains. 'There's no road straight up to the castle to make it harder if an army attacks. You have to follow this road that winds all the way round the town, through three different levels, before you can get to the King's castle. Just stay on it and it will lead you straight there. But don't get distracted and follow another path or you'll end up lost.'

'Wait, aint ye comin with me?' Me voice goes all high-pitched an squeaky cos I don't wanna be left alone, not in a strange city.

Begsy shuffles slightly. 'I've been thinking it's probably best if I go and talk to some old friends, find out if there's any news about Aggy, see if anyone knows who might want to poison Godric.'

'But Begsy, I . . .' He claps me on the shoulder an looks into me eyes.

'You'll be all right, Mold. Besides, we don't have time to lose. We each have to do our jobs.'

'But Aggy always said it was too dangerous here, that's why she never let me come. What if sommink happens?'

'Just keep your head down and keep out of trouble. If you need me send word to the Three Anchors, otherwise I'll meet you tonight back at the stables.'

I gulp down me fear an nod. I can do this. I can do

it fer Aggy. Begsy waves an I watch him head off in the opposite direction. I take a deep breath an start walkin up the road, thinkin about Aggy every step of the way.

It's the smell what does it. Distracts me, I mean. I'm all set on followin the road when this amazin smell, rich an sweet as syrup, drifts towards me an I can't help it. It's like me nose drags me there or sommink.

I can just make out the letters on the front of the buildin where the smell's comin from but I aint never heard of a SWEET SHOPPE fore now. I stare in the fancy glass window an see jars an bowls full of coloured round balls an slabs of sommink brown called CHOC-O-LATE that makes me mouth water an then there's these CAR-A-MELS that almost make me lick the glass.

I could stay here all day just drinkin in the smell, but the woman from the SHOPPE comes out an tells me to get lost.

'We don't want your sort hanging around here,' she snaps, her mouth all pursed up like a shrew. 'You'll bring nothing but bad luck, get off with you!'

I run away, her wicked words ringin in me ears, an I don't pay no mind where I'm goin. Fore long I'm completely lost. I spend ages tryin to find me way back to the main road but it's no good. I can't even follow me nose like usual cos there's too many smells I don't know foggin up me brain an makin me head hurt. I try askin a few people fer directions but they all look at me weird. Like I'm a freak or sommink.

I keep walkin, a sour feelin in me belly, gettin even more lost an fed up. When I spy a deserted alleyway between two big houses I duck inside an slump on the cold cobbles with me back up against the wall just soakin up the quiet an enjoyin five minutes without people starin at me.

Course I used to get strange looks in the Dregs, from the toffs an that at the market, but it wasn't too bad cos they were starin at everyone. Lots of folk ended up in the Dregs cos of the way they looked. Among all the hunchbacks, cripples, an lepers down there I fitted right in.

But here, where everyone is big an blond an normal-lookin I stand out like a sore thumb. I aint seen another soul here with black hair an dark skin let alone a nose like mine. Only thing for it is to get this done quick so I can get home again, back where I belong.

I force meself up on me feet but the sting of vinegar an eggs makes me nostrils prickle. Same second I turn round sommink lands over me head an everythin goes dark.

'Oy!' I yell, tryin to rip off whatever's coverin me face. 'Get off!'

'Shut up!' a voice hisses near me ear but it only makes me shout louder.

'Help!' I yell, slingin out me arms wildly in all directions. I manage to hit sommink squishy with me elbow an hear a muffled swear in return. I take me chance an rip the hessian sack off me face so I can scream again.

'Shut your cake-hole you damn freak!' I look behind me an see Ramsey Bendall, the night watchman from the Dregs, strugglin to his feet clutchin his fat belly.

'What the flamin hell are ye playin at Ramsey? What are you even doin here?'

'Looking for you! Soon as I found out you'd survived the fire I started asking questions. Meg told me where you'd gone after a bit of persuasion.' Ramsey moves towards me, I step backwards, tryin to reach the end of the alley cos the look on his toad-like face is scarin me. 'I've been following you all day, waiting for you to be on your own.'

'But why?'

Ramsey moves in closer. 'Because you're supposed to be dead that's why! If he finds out you escaped and started messing with his plans he'll skin me like a dead skunk!'

'Who will?'

'A certain gentleman who pays a mite better for my skills than King Godric, that's who!'

It slams into place like a ton of bricks. The coins in his purse. The toff at Aggy's. Ramsey'd been workin fer him all along!

'You flamin louse, you set us up didn't ye?'

'A man's gotta make ends meet and you're all scum in the Dregs anyway. What do I care if someone wants to burn down your house and kill you off?' I swing me fist at his face but he dodges back an manages to grab me round the neck. Much as I squirm an fight he don't let go.

'Come on you. I'm handing you over personal.' He twists me arm up behind me back an forces me ahead of him, out of the alley an down the street.

'Get off me ye lousy scumbag!' I shout but Ramsey yanks on me arm an the pain in me shoulder makes me scream.

'Oy! What's all this?' I look up an see a lanky guard in a blue uniform headin towards us.

'Nothing to worry about,' Ramsey says. 'I'm just taking this runaway back where he belongs.'

'He's lyin—'

'Shut up.' He twists me arm again but the guard steps closer an looks at me carefully. The stink of garlic blasts me in the face strong enough to make me nostrils burn.

'Let him go,' he says.

'You're making a mistake . . .'

'I don't think so. Be on your way now before I arrest you for disturbing the peace.'

'Listen, there's a man, a toff, who'll pay good money for him. Help me out and I'll split it with you.'

'I said be off with you!' Garlic-breath shouts, wavin his billy club. Ramsey swears under his breath an lets me go. I watch him walk away while I massage some feelin back into me shoulder.

'Thanks fer that mister.' I smile at the guard.

'That's all right lad. Now, why don't you come with

me?' He locks his hand round my wrist an starts draggin me forward.

'Huh? What fer? I aint done nothin!'

'No you aint, but you're coming with me anyway.'

'That aint fair!' I struggle in his grip but he only squeezes tighter.

'Life aint fair lad. Time you learnt that.' He looks at me an shakes his head. 'I didn't think it was true y'know, I heard a whisper about a Sniffler being seen but I thought it was a joke.'

'I dunno what yer on about. What's a Sniffler?'

'You are, you fool. My old man was a soldier in the Bogger war, he told me about a whole tribe of Snifflers that lived in Pellegarno years ago.'

I feel like I'm frozen in place. There was a tribe? A whole tribe of people just like me? A hundred questions jump into me head but Garlic-breath's still talkin.

'You're gonna make me rich my lad. There's a sea captain who'll pay me a hundred parvels for one of you.'

His words snap me back to reality. I dunno why a sea captain'd pay money fer me but I do know there aint no way I'm goin anywhere. I've gotta save Aggy. She needs me.

I start wrigglin like a fish but the guard's hand is like an iron band an I can't get free.

The sharp acid stink of fear fills the air an a little red-haired kid comes tearin down the street an crashes straight into us, knockin us flat. The boy throws a panicked glance behind him an then he's up an off again.

In the kerfuffle the guard's dropped me arm. He swears an grabs fer me again but I'm too quick fer him. I'm on me feet an runnin an I get swallowed up in a big gang of boys all doin the same. We pelt down street after street an I've no idea where we're headin or why they're all runnin but the need to get as far as I can from Garlic-breath keeps me goin.

We end up stoppin on the banks of a quiet mill stream an I drop me head an pant fer a bit. The other boys pounce on the runty red-headed kid who must have been their prey all along.

They drag him down to the edge of the water though he fights tooth an nail to avoid it.

'DUNK HIM! DUNK HIM!' the lads chant, excitement high in their voices.

'NO! Gerrof me! Gerrof me ye lousy toerags!' He manages to wiggle his arm free an lands a hefty whack on one of his captors. Furious, the bigger lad punches him hard in the stomach an the little kid starts cryin.

I can't help meself. I shouldn't butt in but I can't walk away from him, not after he helped me get away from that guard.

'Oy, why are you pickin on someone half yer size?' I demand, walkin over an grabbin hold of the fella's beefy arm fore he can hit him again. He turns an glares at me but even though he's bigger an me too, I aint scared of him. Well, not much anyways.

'Cos he needs a bath don't he lads?' His friends all cheer in agreement. 'Surely you can smell how much he pongs with that massive great conk of yours?'

The group of boys fall about laughin an pointin at me nose but I ignore em. 'He's only little, why don't ye just leave him alone?'

'Yeah? Well, maybe you're the one who needs a bath?' He nods at his mates an I'm grabbed from behind an bundled towards the water.

'An maybe you wouldn't be so tough if you were on yer own without all yer mates to do yer dirty work?' I yell, strugglin against the others.

Me challenge riles him up, an his mud-brown eyes narrow in my direction. 'All right lads. Let him go.'

The boys push me on to the ground but I get up just in time to get smacked in the chops by a great fist. I go down again, jaw throbbin like a good un.

'Nice one, Duffy!' his mates yell.

'Now, let's dunk that . . .'

'You'll have to do better an that!' I shout, back on me feet an hopin me plan's gonna work cos I really don't think I can take another hit.

Duffy swaggers back over an lines up opposite me. 'You're not getting up again this time boyo,' he says, massagin his fist in readiness.

'Try me,' I say, wavin him on with me hand.

Duffy growls an charges like a bull. I bite me lip an try an hold me nerve as he gets closer an closer. Finally, at the last second I dodge to me right, bring me fist up into his gut an then stick me leg out. Duffy goes flyin straight over it an into the stream with a huge splash.

His friends stand there with their mouths gapin open so I dive forward an grab the little kid from their grasp.

'Come on!' I yell an we pelt off into the streets. We duck down a couple of alleys, runnin fast as we can, then pull up behind a low brick wall by some bins to catch our breath an look behind.

'They're comin after us!' the little fella hisses. 'I can hear em.'

'We're in trouble then cos I can't run no more,' I gasp.

'We'll have to hide then,' the boy says an he shoves me backwards into the pile of rubbish next to the bins then crawls in next to me.

I have to hold me breath cos the stink of rottin cabbage an dead things near makes me throw up. I can hear shoutin in the alley, Duffy's voice hollerin, boys trampin past us but finally the noise fades away. Everythin goes quiet.

The kid scrambles up an makes sure the coast is clear. He's walkin awkward though an I can see he's in pain.

'Are ye all right?' I climb out from the trash pile an brush the mouldy cabbage leaves an fish heads off me clothes. 'Are ye hurt?'

'Nah,' he sniffs. 'I'm all right. I've been hit harder than

that before now.' He straightens an stares up at me with shinin green eyes. 'Flamin Nora that wasn't half brilliant what you did! I aint never seen anyone stand up to Duffy like that before.'

'Aye, well, I don't like bullies,' I tell him but I think that Duffy fella might have been half right. It wasn't just the rubbish that stunk so bad. The kid needed a bath sommink fierce. He smells like someone had thrown him in a cesspit an left him there fer a week.

'Where'd ye learn to fight like that?'

'Ye don't grow up in the Dregs without learnin a thing or two,' I tell him.

'The Dregs? Cor, you've come a long way aint ye?'

'Aye. Listen, I don't suppose y'know how to get to the castle do ye?' I step back, away from his pong, but he stays glued to me side like a limpet.

'Course I do. I work there don't I? I'll show ye if ye want?' He grabs hold of me hand an starts walkin, draggin me behind him. 'What do they call ye in the Dregs then?'

'Mold, they call me Mold but look . . . ye can just tell me the way, y'know,' I try, hopin to get rid of the little tyke an the pong surroundin him. 'Ye don't have to take me there.'

'Course I do. I owe ye for saving me and Fergus always pays his debts.' He grips me hand even tighter. I sigh an let him carry on. I reckon he's lyin about workin in the castle but as long as he knows the way I don't suppose it matters.

Chapter 6

Fergus don't stop talkin the whole way an the smell of him only gets riper as the day gets warmer. I listen with half an ear while he chatters on an make sure I keep me head down. I can do without any more trouble.

We keep walkin, up through the second level an when we reach the third I'm gawkin good an proper cos it's like a different world almost. There's paved roads up here fer all their fancy horse-drawn carriages an tree-lined paths fer folk to wander down.

'So, any news on the King?' I ask when Fergus takes a breath. 'I heard he got poisoned.'

'He did. They're laying bets down Fortune Alley about how long he's got.'

'And?'

'A few days is the best bet. Molly the chambermaid overheard the healer.'

I let out a breath. 'Then there's still time to save him? That's good news.'

'I aint so sure. I've heard a few people down the market say we'd be better off with a new king.'

'Aint so long ago people thought King Godric was the bee's knees.'

'Well it's been a long while since he saved us from the Boggers and all he's done lately is bleed us dry while he sails round the Seven Isles in the lap of luxury.' Fergus says it in a funny posh voice that makes me laugh.

'Who'd be the new king if he did die?' I ask, wonderin if maybe they was the one who'd paid the toff.

'Well, his son Prince Iric's next in line but he's still too young to rule.'

So no point in him doin it then I guess. 'So what'd happen?'

Fergus shrugs. 'Someone'd help him I suppose, till he was old enough. He's got a few uncles on his dead ma's side but most likely his Uncle Nash'd be regent I think. He's been sick with the lung rot since the Bogger wars but he helps his brother Godric out a bit an he's the only one who gives a fig fer the common folk.'

The path gets steeper an I stop talkin an save me puff fer walkin. I figure we must be near the castle now. I flamin hope so anyway. Seems like I've spent half the day runnin away from people an gettin bashed an now I'm tired an hot an hungry an I aint done nothin I'm supposed to yet.

'Are we nearly there?' I ask Fergus, stoppin fer a quick breath.

'Yeah, the gate's just up ahead.' He points a filthy finger to the left but I aint listenin any more, just sniffin.

The stink of curdled milk fills me nostrils, just a whiff but enough so's I know it's him an I don't care what Begsy said about danger an keepin out of sight, I can't let this chance go.

'Oy, Mold! Where are ye goin?' Fergus shouts after me but I don't stop runnin. I follow the scent trail like a dog after a fox till I catch sight of the toff standin over by the high walls that surround the castle havin some sort of argument with another man.

Maybe it's the man he works fer? Maybe I can find out who it is? I sneak closer, keepin meself tucked out of sight round the corner an pressed tight against the wall till I can overhear what they're sayin.

'. . . you lost him?' The toff's voice is furious. Anger, bitter an harsh, rises off him in waves.

'It wasn't my fault.' I recognize Ramsey's whiny voice straight off. I'd been so focused on the putrid stink off that toff I hadn't even noticed his vinegary pong.

'I see.'

'But he's alive and he's here in the city. Some guard took him off me, I tried to tell him about you . . .'

'You mentioned me?' That voice is so cold I get goosebumps all over.

'Well . . . no . . . not really . . . I mean . . .' Ramsey stammers, the stink of his fear risin in the air.

'I warned you what would happen if you ever spoke of me.' There's a muffled yelp, then a scream an then silence.

I'm almost afeared to peek round the wall but I do it anyway. Ramsey's lyin on the floor unconscious. His mouth is drippin with blood an next to him is a small, fleshy, pink lump . . . a tongue-shaped lump . . .

A shiver runs up me spine.

'Mold? Where are ye?' Fergus yells. I freeze against the wall. 'Mold!' Does the toff know me name? I don't dare look an see if the toff heard. I don't dare breathe.

I can hear footsteps, quiet footsteps an they're comin my way. Suddenly I wish I'd taken Begsy's advice an stayed well away from this man.

The footsteps are gettin closer. I can't breathe but me heart pounds like a drum, so loud I reckon he might hear it.

His shadow looms onto the path an I'm swamped by the sour stench that rises off him like a cloud an then it's gone. He's gone. I can feel me knees near collapse with relief watchin him stride away.

'Mold!' Fergus runs over, a big smile on his face. 'What you doing round here? The gate's that way.'

'I thought I saw someone I knew, that's all,' I tell him, keepin the wobble out of me voice somehow.

'An did ye?'

'Nah, it was a mistake, that's all.'

'Well, come on then, we're nearly there.' He goes to take me hand but I pull away.

'It's all right. I can get there meself.' I reckon it's best if I'm on me own from now on. I don't want Fergus gettin caught up with all the trouble that's after me. Not after seein what that toff done to Ramsey fer no more an passin on bad news. 'Thanks fer bringin me though.'

'S'all right.' Fergus wipes his nose on his sleeve but makes no move to leave.

'So . . . see you around I guess?'

'What ye gonna do up at the castle anyway?' he asks. 'Are ye waiting fer someone?'

'I'm waitin fer you to go away,' I mutter.

'That's a good one. You're funny.' He grins at me, showin off the gaps in his top gum. 'I'm glad you come to the city, Mold, whatever reason it is. Aint no one ever stood up fer me before. It's like you're me very best friend aint it?'

'No it aint, not really,' I mutter, squirmin a bit under his desperate gaze.

'It is! Oh, go on. No one ever wants to be best friends with me, I dunno why. I'd be a really good best friend. I know the castle cook an she gives me all the best pies an biscuits. I'd let ye have some if ye were my best friend.'

'Look, I can't, I've got stuff to do.'

'What stuff?' I can tell he aint gonna leave less I make him.

'Aint none of yer business is it?' I keep me voice hard an ignore the wounded look on his little face. 'Now go on, get lost will ye?'

'Yeah. All right then. I got stuff to do an all y'know.' He sniffs, shrugs, an wanders away slowly. I feel like a louse but I'm doin it fer him aint I?

I put Fergus outta me head an walk the final steps up the path an through the gate an then I'm in the royal courtyard an I can see the castle at last, sittin right on top of the hill with a view of the whole city.

Me mouth gapes open like a codfish. It's bigger an all the Dregs put together with fine red stone walls, oak doors, tall towers, an real glass windows. I aint never seen a house so big, I bet ye could lose yer way in there an still be wanderin about a week later.

All the relief I feel at makin it this far disappears when I try an figure out me chances of gettin inside cos they aint good. The doors are all guarded, even the roof's got blue guards patrollin along the top.

I tie me neckerchief over me nose an try an blend into the crowds while I stroll round the courtyard lookin fer a way in. I get distracted from me plans by a hunched old lady carryin a tray of hot rolls an I wish I'd thought to bring some of Meg's food with me cos it's long past breakfast an me stomach's emptier an a bucket with a hole in it. I drink in the smell as if it can fill me up, but under the scent of rich, roasted beef an onions I pick up the faintest stink of garlic an it aint comin from the meat.

It don't take long to find the cause. I follow me nose an catch sight of Garlic-breath makin his way through the crowds.

I can't let him spot me.

I spin round an see a line of carts movin along the edge of the castle an through a big wooden gate. I hurry over an manage to nab hold of a passin wagon. I climb over the side an hide among the sheep, holdin me breath against the stink.

A young lad jumps on the bench with a mug of tea he hands to the driver who must be his granddad or sommink. The old fella starts wafflin like there's no tomorrow. I peer round the side of the wagon an spot a side door in the castle, seems like workers an delivery men use it an it might just be me best chance of gettin in. I'm about to jump out when some of Granddad's words seep through.

'. . . Snifflers they were called but no one ever saw them. They hid deep in the forests and folk thought they were evil spirits and made the sign to warn off bad luck.' There's a pause while he slurps his tea. 'They were barely ever seen properly until King Godric needed them to fight his war. I saw a few of them being dragged along by ropes into the swamps to find the Boggers. They were strange-looking I tell you with their dark hair and skin and these great big noses . . .'

'Yeah, yeah, Granddad. Shall I get you a bun to go with

your tea?' His grandson might not be interested but I am. I'm drinkin in every word. I wish Aggy an Begsy hadn't kept all this a secret, I could have gone lookin for me tribe, maybe even found me ma, found out why she left me.

'You sit yer bum down and listen to some history! Those Snifflers could find anything with those noses of theirs but it didn't do them any good because the Boggers killed them for what they did. The whole tribe was wiped out and never seen again.'

'What's all this got to do with me, Granddad?'

I can't breathe proper. They were dead? All dead?

That's why Aggy never told me.

What was the point of tellin me about a dead family?

The granddad tuts loudly. 'Cos, you blithering berk, word is that one of them's been seen in the city.'

'Sounds daft if you ask me.'

'No one's asking you. Just keep your eye out for him, Milo. I heard he'd be worth money to some.'

I snap out of me daze an climb outta the cart quiet as I can. This is me best chance of gettin in unnoticed, while the guards are all millin around, drinkin mugs of tea, scoffin barmcakes, an chattin up the maids. I can't waste it thinkin about a dead tribe, not if I'm gonna save Aggy. An I have to save Aggy. She's all the family I got.

A big fella wearin a blood-smeared apron takes a large crate of dead rabbits off the back of his cart an I dart in, grab another box an follow him. I keep me eyes down, keep walkin an hope I get away with it.

Soon as I'm in the massive kitchen I dump the box on the table an head fer the doorway only I get snagged by the ear.

'I hope these rabbits are fresh this time? I won't be having rotten rabbits in my kitchen.' I wince with pain an peer up at a massive great whale of a woman with warts on her nose an rotten, black teeth. 'Who are you? You're not Aldo's boy!'

'He's sick, I'm . . . I'm just fillin in,' I try, hopin she'll let go of me ear but no chance. She yanks me after her, back out the door.

'Aldo! Is this lad with you?'

The butcher turns round an stares at me. 'No. Never seen him before.'

'I knew it. You were trying to sneak in weren't you?' She lets go of me ear but only so she can grab me shoulders an shake me like a rag doll. 'I'm fed up of you guttersnipes sneaking into my kitchen and stealing all my cakes and pastries. Sick of it!' she roars, spittle flyin in me face.

'I aint stole nothin, get offa me.'

'I'm calling the guard this time.'

'No!' I yell, strugglin even more cos if the guards are anything like Garlic-breath I'm done fer. 'I aint taken nothin, honest, just let me go.'

'Yeah, let him go Mildred.' The cook stops shakin me. We turn to see where the voice came from. It's flamin Fergus. I wait fer her to fly at him an let rip but she just smiles. If anythin she looks even uglier, but it is a smile.

'Fergus, do you know this boy?'

'This is Mold. He's me best friend, aint ya?' Fergus smiles at me.

I gulp. 'Aye.'

The cook lets go of me an I scramble out of her reach just in case. 'What's he doing stealing my pies then?'

'He aint stealing nothin are ye, Mold?' Fergus asks me calm as can be. I shake me head from side to side. 'I told him to meet me outside but he must have got confused. Probably smelt your cookin and couldn't resist comin in.'

Mildred peers at me, suspicion glintin in her eyes but Fergus beams at her and finally she shrugs. 'I'll let him off this time, seeing as he's your friend. Now come with me and I'll get you some of the buns I made fresh this morning.'

'You know I'd walk a hundred miles for some of your buns, Mildred. No one can bake like you.' Fergus gives me a quick wink an points over at the gate. I head over there quick as I can an Fergus meets me there a few minutes later carryin a brown paper bag.

'Blimey, Fergus, how'd you manage that? I thought she was gonna kill me.' I'm feelin even worse now fer bein so mean to him earlier.

'Oh, Mildred'll do anythin for me, I helped her out once so she owes me.'

'Well, thanks.'

'That's all right. I still owe you for saving me from Duffy.' Fergus offers me a bun. I grab one an take a bite, then another an another till it's all gone. 'Good, aint they?'

I nod me head. 'Amazin.'

'You was lucky I was there to save you, Mildred could have pounded you to a pulp.'

'She tried.' I rub me ear which still stings. 'Blimey, I never thought it'd be so hard to get into the castle.'

'Why'd ye wanna get in so bad?'

I sigh an decide to tell him a small part of the truth. 'I need to see the King. It's important.'

'I can get ye in to see the King,' Fergus says as if it's the easiest thing in the world.

'Ye can? D'you really work in the castle then?'

'I told ye I did, didn't I?' He puffs out his chest proudly. 'I'm the royal privy pipe cleaner.'

The reason behind Fergus' dodgy aroma becomes clear an me belly turns over at the idea of wadin though any pipe that smells worse an him. 'Ye wanna take me into the sewer?'

'It's easier than trying to fight Mildred and the guard all by yerself.'

I know he's right but I still reckon I'd rather take me chance with Mildred an Garlic-breath than the privies.

Chapter 7

I imagined the sewer would be a terrible, horrible, disgustin, filth-ridden, scum-covered nightmare of a place but I was wrong.

It was much, MUCH worse.

Fergus skips through the manky pipes, his bare feet splashin through the brown, fetid, mulchy water that rises past his ankles without a murmur, while I stagger an groan an retch every step of the way. I dread to think what it'd be like down here without the peg an the cloth Fergus fixed over me nose fore I finally agreed to come down here.

'Cor, you don't half make a fuss,' he says, turnin round, the lamp in his hand showin me far more than I wanna see.

'How can ye bear it?' I cough. 'It's disgustin down here.'

'It aint that bad, you should see the public sewer, that's proper nasty. They've got rats down there as long as me arm!'

'Oh I aint bothered by rats, there's loads of em in the Dregs.'

'Well, I bet they aint got Yurg in the Dregs. They had em in the public sewer last year and three people got killed.'

'Yurg? I aint never heard of em.'

'They're like these big slug creatures, they stick on to the ceiling and never move. Every so often they burst open and spew out millions of grubs that eat everything they can find. They'll gnaw a person down to the bone in minutes they reckon. When the grubs have finished eating they go back to their Yurg and get swallowed back up. Their poop is the Yurg's supper.' Fergus grins at me while I swallow down a mouthful of bile.

'Shut up, Fergus, will ye? Bad enough down here without hearin horror stories!'

'It's all right, Mold. I been down here three years and I've never seen one. Sides all they do is open the sluice gate and wash the grubs out.'

I shudder an change the subject sharpish. 'How d'ya end up in this job anyway?'

'They send a load of orphans over from the workhouse every year to do the jobs no one else wants to do.' Fergus sniffs an wipes his nose on the back of his hand. 'Soggy Joe's place where we all live is a bit of a madhouse but least down here it's nice and quiet and no one tries to beat me up.'

I have to give Fergus credit fer lookin at the bright side of things. Not many'd find it in a place like this.

'And I'm proper good at me job y'know. Since I been cleaning the pipes there aint been no complaints or nothing!' He puffs out his chest like he's proud as punch. 'Go on, Mold, climb up and see how clean it is!'

'Er . . . no don't worry Fergus. I believe ye.' His little face falls so flat I feel like I've kicked him in the guts or sommink. 'Oh, all right then but just quickly,' I say.

Fergus beams at me an I climb up the metal ladder inside the pipe fast as I can. The top of the tunnel widens out an I can see there's a few different privies all leadin to this pipe. It's strangely echoey up here an I can hear voices driftin down. A woman naggin at her kid, a man hummin a song, an then I hear a voice that makes me pause.

'. . . you seen anyone like that Jim?' It's a bit muffled but I'm almost sure I recognize it. I cling to the rungs, waitin to hear more.

'A kid with a massive nose?'

'He's worth a lot of money. If you see him let me know and I'll make sure you get a cut.' It's Garlic-breath.

'I could do with one, the wages King Godric pays aint enough to keep a flea!'

'Well keep your eyes peeled then, this could be a decent haul.'

Silence fer a minute an then over me head comes a stream of yellow pee that hits the wall an splashes in me hair. I climb down the ladder so fast I nearly fall.

'Clean innit?' Fergus says.

'Aye. Very clean,' I agree through gritted teeth, the

stench of pee still pricklin in me nostrils.

We keep walkin. Fergus chatters on but I aint really listenin. I'm too busy worryin.

'Is it much further?' I ask, cos if I stay in Westenburg much longer I reckon I'm gonna end up either sold or dead an that can't happen. Aggy needs me.

'Nah, not really. Round the corner are the pipes from the royal family's privies and that's where we'll find what we want.'

'Thank the stars fer that. I dunno how much more of this I can take.'

'What's so important about visiting the King anyway?' he asks.

'I just need to see him, that's all.'

'You can tell me y'know. I'm good at keeping secrets and sides we're best friends now, aint we?' He turns a gappy smile on me. I can't help smilin back at him. Sommink about him tugs at me heart but can I really trust him? He'd saved me from Garlic-breath an Mildred an gave me a way into the castle but . . . I've only known him five minutes. I can't tell him the truth yet. It aint safe fer him or me.

'Look, Fergus, it's really important I find out who poisoned the King, so I just need to see him fer a minute, all right?'

'But they already caught the one who poisoned him, I saw her being dragged into the dungeons last night.'

'You saw Aggy? Where? How was she?' I can't keep the worry from me voice.

'I was up the maintenance tunnel.' He points out a round

metal door in the pipe wall. 'I go up there sometimes when I'm bored cos it goes past the dungeons where me mate works. Why d'you care about some old lady anyway?'

'Cos . . . look, she didn't do it, she's been set up see an I have to save her.'

Fergus watches me fer a minute, then grins. 'Cor, you mean it's like a proper rescue mission an everything!' His squinty eyes gleam with excitement. 'I can help ya Mold, I'm real good at helpin. Can I be like yer partner?'

'It's all right. I don't need a partner.'

'Oh, go on, I'd be the best partner ever,' he begs. I can't let him though. It's too dangerous.

'Honest, Fergus . . .'

'Listen though, wait, cos I'm real fast y'know, look, watch me run.' He pelts off down the tunnel, little legs flyin through the sludge. I'm trudgin after him, shakin me head an tryin not to puke when a loud crackin sounds above me head.

I look up an just make out a mud-brown slug-like shape ripplin an writhin on the ceilin, drippin some foul ooze into the tunnel. I walk faster but a minute later I can feel slime drippin onto me head.

'Urgh, oy Fergus, what's all this gunky stuff?'

He bounds back towards me an holds his lamp up higher. His face drops an his hand trembles, makin the light waver in front of me eyes.

'Run,' he breathes, turnin around an speedin away up the sewer. 'Now!'

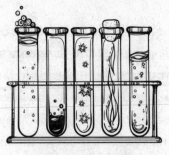

Chapter 8

I pelt after Fergus, catchin him up after a few strides.

'What is it? What are we runnin fer?'

'They're gonna kill us!' he breathes, his face white.

'What? What's gonna kill us?'

'The Yurg!'

'Ye mean they was hatchin? Just now? An they're gonna eat us? Blimey Fergus, I thought ye said it was safe down here!' I look behind me, the walls seem to be movin, a dark shadow ripplin towards us like a wave. I run faster, heart thumpin like a drum.

'They never got in here before, never.'

'Well they're here now . . . so how do we flush out the sewer?'

'There's a wheel, up ahead.'

'How far away?' I swing me head round again, the walls shimmer, alive with the march of thousands of black bugs.

'About fifty yards.'

I stop talkin. Rip the cloth an peg from me nose an cram em in me pocket. Don't care about the smell any more. No breath to waste. Head down. Arms pumpin. Focused only on gettin to the flamin wheel fore I get eat.

A splash an a squeal force me to stop an I have to turn round, go back an yank Fergus out of the sludge. He's gone flyin over what looks like a dead cow's head an he's sobbin an shakin now, drippin with filth.

'We gotta go,' I insist. Fergus nods an starts runnin again but I can see he's flaggin an I aint sure how long he's gonna last. I turn round again an see the grubs surge over the cow head like locusts. While I watch they devour the head, crunchin through everythin from flesh to bone an leavin nothin behind.

A few seconds later an that could have been Fergus.

It might still be Fergus if he don't hurry up.

'Come on Fergus, I thought ye said you were fast?' I yell. 'If yer gonna be me partner you'd better be faster an that!'

'I am fast, Mold. Honest I am.' He finds the energy from somewhere an starts catchin me up.

'Not bad Fergus, come on, keep goin.'

He puffs an pants but his little legs keep movin. 'There it is!' Fergus points to a break in the pipe about ten yards ahead. It aint far but I can hear the bugs scrabblin an scritchin across the walls an I'm not sure we're gonna make it.

I force me legs to keep goin an duck into the alcove just ahead of Fergus.

'Turn. The. Wheel,' Fergus pants, slumpin on the floor, his face white an ghostly. Too exhausted to even move.

I grab hold of the big iron wheel an just about manage to heave it round though it wrenches me shoulders.

'The flamin thing's all rusty!' I shout at Fergus.

'Keep goin Mold. Ye have to open the gates all the way to flush it out.' Fergus orders, peerin round the corner to check fer grubs.

'So the water'll wash the Yurg away?'

'Nah,' he gets up an helps me turn the wheel. 'They're stuck fast but the grubs'll wash out to sea and without them the Yurgs'll shrivel up an die.'

We keep pushin on the wheel, drivin it round an round as fast as we can but it aint fast enough cos the bugs are comin. I can hear em on the walls an now they're scramblin into the alcove.

'They're coming Mold! What we gonna do?'

Me mind races, tryin to think up a plan. I remember how they used to smoke out buildins in the Dregs to get rid of the roaches. 'Here, take this.' I hand him the cloth I was wearin over me nose. 'Set it on fire, quick.'

Fergus gulps an follows me instructions, usin the oil lamp to set it alight. I'm hopin the fire an smoke'll keep em off us fer long enough to open the gates.

It works fer a little while an I haul on the wheel like a

mad thing but then the fire starts to die an a few of em sneak through. The soft-shelled insects scramble like a tiny army towards us an now they're close to the lamp I can see em proper fer the first time. Each one's no bigger an me finger, but their mouths take up near half their bodies an are filled with nothin but teeth, tiny, sharp an serrated as knives. More start droppin off the ceilin an a few of em land in me hair.

I can feel em bitin at me flesh an the urge to yell an brush em away's almost too strong but I somehow manage to keep me hands on the wheel, turnin it round an round spite the blood drippin into me eyes.

Fergus starts screamin as bugs swarm into the alcove an crawl up his legs. I can see more an more of em followin behind like a carpet of death.

I summon every ounce of strength I've got an give an almighty tug on the wheel. It swings round an locks in to place.

Nothin happens.

Panic thunders through me as I imagine the horror of bein eaten alive in this stinkin sewer but then the sweet, wet smell of the river hits me followed by an almighty roar. Water floods into the sewer like a tidal wave, a huge wall of freezin river that fills up the alcove in seconds.

I grab Fergus's hand an pull him up with me to the ladder that hangs above us an we cling on fer dear life while the water thunders past, draggin every rotten grub away with it.

Fergus an me shiver on the ladder waitin fer the water to drain away, only our heads above the water now. I can feel one last grub tearin at me scalp so I lift a numb hand to brush it away only me other hand slips off the ladder an I end up fallin into the water.

I swallow great mouthfuls of river an I'm chokin . . . chokin . . . smackin gainst the walls of the alcove, the only thing savin me from bein dragged away.

I fight against the pull of the water an try an find me way to the surface, try to find the ladder again, try not to flamin well drown . . . a small hand slips into mine an yanks me up, me other hand finds the ladder an I cling to the rungs, just about managin to pull me head out of the flood an get some air into me lungs.

Long minutes later the water finally recedes an Fergus an I climb back down into the sewer, drenched, bleedin, an shakin. Me legs wobble so much I end up slumpin on to the sewer floor. Lucky fer me it's been washed clear of all the scum, only the last bits of river remain in great, muddy puddles.

I gulp away the last bits of fear an terror an try to calm down. I'm alive. Spite the grubs an the water I'm still alive. Spite the blood an the bruises an the pain.

I look over at Fergus, blood drippin down his legs an arms, snot an tears stainin his little face, misery leakin from every pore.

'I'm sorry, Mold!' he bursts out. 'I didn't know they was down here honest, I never meant for ye to nearly get eaten by bugs.'

'Don't be daft. It aint your fault, I know that.'

Fergus rubs the tears away with his hands an gives me a small smile. 'Really? Yer still me best friend then?' I nod. 'An I'm still yer partner? Like ye said?'

'You saved me didn't ye? Pulled me out of the water? Course we're friends Fergus, and partners. Honest.' I grab Fergus an pull him to me fer a quick hug. He squeezes me back as if he's never had a hug before an then I realize it might well be true so I let him stay where he is a bit longer. 'Sides, I reckon it might all have been worth it. Ye needed that bath fer sure.'

Fergus snorts an lets me go. 'I aint been this clean fer years.'

I smile. He still pongs if I'm honest, like the smell's embedded in his skin somehow, but it's better an it was so I aint complainin. 'So, ye gonna show me where to go now or what? I really need to see the King.'

He nods an I get to me feet an we set off back the way we come, limpin like wounded soldiers.

'Mold? D'you want me to come with ye and help?'

'Nah. I don't want ye gettin in trouble.'

'Shall I wait here for ye then?'

'No! I aint comin back down here again. Not fer

nothin. I'll sneak out the back door or sommink. Just lock up behind me an I'll meet ye in front of the castle later, all right?'

He nods an then points to a tunnel on the right. 'That's the one, Mold. The King's own privy pipe.'

'Brilliant. Thanks Fergus.' I grip hold of the ladder an start climbin.

'Mold?' Fergus's voice follows me. 'Ye will come back won't ya?' I peer down at his little white face an see the fear an loneliness in his squinty green eyes.

'I'll be back Fergus. I promise.'

I'm rewarded by a beamin grin an then he's gone an I'm finally on me own, clingin to the inside of the King's privy pipe hopin that somehow it's all gonna be worth it.

Chapter 9

At the top of the pipe there's the wooden privy an a metal catch underneath that'll let me open the whole seat an push it up out of the way. Fergus said it's in case it gets blocked or needs to be replaced.

I keep an ear out fer a few seconds to make sure no one's in the room. Then I open the catch an pull meself up. I crawl through the hole an fall with a thunk on the hard tile floor breathin in the clean scent of freshly laundered cotton. I scramble to me feet an stare at the shiny copper bath, the white linen towels, the large silver-framed mirror on the wall, an the reality of where I am sinks in.

I've made it. I've crawled through the stinkin sewer, escaped flesh-eatin grubs an ended up in the King's own privy chamber. I tremble in the toasty warmth, hardly believin me luck. I've got much further than I ever imagined thanks to Fergus an his stinky job, but I know I aint outta danger yet. If I get caught in here I'm proper done fer.

I look round fer somewhere to hide an see a curtain in the far wall. I pull it back carefully an stare inside. It must be the King's dressin room cos there's fancy clothes hangin on a long rail an a chest of drawers with brushes an combs an razors on. I look down at me own soppin wet an stinky clothes an a mad idea comes into me head.

I take off me wet togs, throw em in the wash basket an rummage in the drawers till I find the simplest, oldest trews an tunic that I can. I have to fold up the bottoms an arms a bit an wrap a belt round me to keep em up but it's worth it to be warm an dry.

I find a dirty apron in the washin basket an tie it round me middle, comb me fingers through me hair to tidy it up a bit an I reckon, if no one looks too close, I might just pass fer a castle servant.

Now fer the hard bit. I take a deep breath an head over to the door an listen, I can hear a soft voice but I can't quite make out what it's sayin through the wood.

Carefully, I ease the door open a tiny bit an peer through the gap. I can see a great four poster bed an I can make out the shape of a body lyin neath the blankets. That must be Godric.

Standin next to the bed is a woman in a long black gown, her grey hair all tied up in a knot. She's got a cup full of sommink in her hand an she's tryin to spoon the contents into Godric's mouth. Most of it dribbles out the side an stains the cloth an she swears under her breath.

There's a knock on the door an she puts the cup down an removes the cloth fore she calls em in.

'Ah, Healer Brawn. Any success with our latest trials?'

'I'm afraid not.' The new visitor is a small stooped man dressed in the same long black gown an smellin of herbs an oil.

She curses under her breath. 'Has the poisoner offered any information?'

'She's still denying all allegations.' Aggy! They were talkin bout Aggy!

'But didn't they find the bottle with her mark on it by the King's bed and a parvel in her possession?'

So that's how he'd done it the stinkin louse.

'She says she was framed but Lord Nash claims he has evidence that she's part of a rebel group from the Dregs.'

A rebel group? What a load of old rot.

'Perhaps I should ask her myself?'

'Yourself? But Madam, surely the dungeons are not a fitting place for a lady.'

'They are fitting for a healer however. Now come along.' She marches off an the little man scurries out behind her.

Fore I can change me mind, I push the door open, run into the room an over to the King, tangled in a mess of sweat-soaked sheets. His handsome face is white an clammy an I can smell his breath, sour with sickness an rot. I can tell he aint got long just by lookin at him. The flesh has fallen from his bones an they stick out, sharp as a knife. Deep black circles surround his eyes like great bruises an he moans an trembles in his fevered sleep.

He'll die soon. I can smell it on him like a shadow. He's only a few days left at the most an when he dies they'll string my Aggy up an watch her dangle on the rope. They'll both be in their graves by Sunday at the latest. The only thing that can save em is me.

I step closer, nerves scrabblin in me belly like claws. Could I really do this?

Only one way to find out.

I bend down, close me eyes an inhale. The different scents mingle in me head.

Sweat . . . beeswax . . . smoke from the fire . . . umm . . . lavender in the sheets . . . poppy syrup fer the pain . . . willow bark fer his fever . . .

There has to be more. I take another breath, deeper this time till I can almost taste it.

There . . . that's it . . . the cloyin sweetness of henbane . . . an dogweed . . . sharp like rotten limes . . .

That aint it though, there's more, sommink deeper, hidin beneath the others like a grotbug.

Bitterness . . . harsh an strong . . . acrid . . . it burns me nose, I can taste it in me throat . . . The name tugs at me, I can feel it there in me mind, the piece of the puzzle that I need . . .

A picture flashes into me brain . . . me sittin on the floor in the basement, playin with a ragged old stuffed dog . . . sommink falls on the floor . . . dark black an shiny, I reach out me hand but Aggy shrieks an snatches it away . . . No, Mold she shouts not the . . . gurdiskar! The final ingredient is gurdiskar root.

All them years under Aggy's table meant I know these ingredients, I recognize their smells.

Maybe it is all true about me bein a Sniffler? All them clever healers aint been able to figure out the poison but I have. Perhaps me nose is a blessin after all? It might save the King an Aggy an everythin!

The King shudders in his sleep an moans. I grab a cloth from the bowl of water next to his bed an rest it on his sweat-soaked forehead.

'Please don't die,' I whisper to the King. 'I'm gonna find a cure. You just need to hang on a bit longer, all right?'

'What in heaven's name are you doing?' The voice behind me is haughty an furious. I spin round and see a middle-aged man standin in the doorway, a toff of some sort.

'N . . . n . . . nothin . . .' I stammer cos this don't look good. Even I can see that. 'I swear mister. I was just tryin to help.'

He glares at me. I gulp, spot a tray of cups an bowls on the side table an I pick it up as if I really am a servant an that tray's the only reason I'm in here.

The nobleman glides past me. He reeks of menthol an camphor with the faintest hint of wine on his breath. He observes the King fer a moment, watches the shallow rise an fall of his chest, reaches out his hand to check the cloth I'd put on his head an seems to relax.

'Stay away from the King, boy,' he says, smoothin down the cloth carefully, exposin his wrist an the hint of a birthmark. 'He's very sick, the last thing he needs is "help" from a servant.'

Me hands tremble. The crockery clatters on the shakin tray. 'Yes sir. Sorry sir.'

'Off you go then, be back about your work,' he says, wavin at the door. I can't believe me ears. I've got away with it! I leave the room sharpish fore he can change his mind, an sag against the wall fer a minute. Talk about a close shave. I can near feel the razor nick me neck.

At least the hardest bit's over. All I have to do now is get out of this place fore anythin else can go wrong.

I set off down the corridor, head down, tray firmly grasped in front of me like some sort of shield. A man rushes down the corridor towards me. A man in snakeskin boots.

The rest of his clothes have changed from before, they're all fine silks an velvets now an he's covered up his tattoo with powder but I know it's him all the same. I'd know him anywhere from the the sour stink that oozes from his every pore.

He barely glances at me as he passes, I suppose he thinks I'm just another servant but I stop in me tracks an stare at his back. He pauses outside the King's door an then knocks.

Me brain finally snaps back into action an I start walkin again. I'm tempted to throw the tray an just leg it but I don't. I walk fast though. Down the corridor an away from the tattooed toff.

I'm nearly out of sight now, nearly at the stairs but I can't help wonderin what he's doin at the King's door. I turn round, hopin fer a quick peek.

He's standin, still waitin outside the door but he must feel me lookin cos he turns his head real quick an when he sees me a sudden spark of recognition flashes in his eyes.

'You, boy! Wait there.' His voice rings with command but I keep walkin, faster an faster cursin meself fer a curious fool. I head down the first set of stairs an through an archway into the next corridor which has a row of closed doors along one side.

'Stop I say!'

I dump the tray an try the first handle. Locked. The second. Locked.

I can smell him comin.

The third. Locked. The fourth. Locked.

He'll be here any second. He'll see me an then he'll take out his knife an . . .

The fifth . . . Open.

I rush in an close the door quiet as I can. I take a quick

look round the chamber an it's empty, thank the stars. I check the keyhole, if I can just lock the door I'll be safe, he'll never find me, but there's no key. Nothin to stop him gettin in.

I can hear him rattlin the other doors. I've got only a minute or two fore he gets here. Do I try an block the door? The furniture looks too heavy fer me to shift. So I should hide then? Under the bed? In the wardrobe? No, don't be stupid, Mold. Too obvious.

He's nearly here. Blood pounds in me head.

Then it comes to me, a scent in the air an I know what to do.

Chapter 10

The door creaks open.

'Boy?' he calls quietly. His snakeskin boots make only the slightest sound as he pads around the room. 'I know you're in here. There's no point hiding.'

The wardrobe door squeaks.

'I'm curious though. What is it you think you can do here in the city? No one will believe anything a Dregger brat has to say.'

I'm guessin he's lookin under the bed now. Only place left is behind the curtains . . .

'You should never have come here boy, I am more dangerous than you can ever imagine.' His voice is so close now, as he reaches the window, almost directly in me ear.

Me knees are tremblin, me fingers strainin as they try an keep their grip.

'You can't be allowed to spoil my plans, I warn you now . . .'

'Hello?' Another voice in the room, deep an cross. 'What are you doing in my bedchamber?'

'Ah, apologies. My purse was stolen and I saw the brat run in here. I was merely searching for him.'

'Really?' The voice sounds suspicious. 'Well there aren't that many places he could hide, are there?'

'Indeed. No, I guess he must have escaped somehow.' I can hear the irritation leakin through his words. 'I'll leave you then and continue my search elsewhere. He won't escape me, I can assure you of that.'

The door clicks closed an I let out a huge breath. If that toff had looked out the window he might have spotted me. I'm clingin to the wall beside it, forty foot in the air, too scared to look down.

'Stupid oaf,' the voice in the room mutters an I suddenly realize what it means. I can't climb back in if there's someone there.

Five minutes ago when I smelled the fresh air an climbed out the window it had seemed like a good idea. Now, hands bleedin from graspin the rock an about five seconds from losin their grip entirely, I think it's the worst idea I ever had.

Half fallin, scrabblin fer handholds, I slide down the wall hopin there'll be an open window I can climb through. By the time I tumble through the only open window two floors down I've lost three fingernails, scraped half me knee off, an nearly died of a heart attack twice.

I lie on the floor, not quite believin I'm still alive.

A foot nudges me.

'Well, will you look who it is?' I look upwards. Garlic-breath stands over me, his eyes gleamin, an me heart sinks. How is this fair? 'My lovely little moneypot, crawled through the window straight into the guard's room, how perfect is that?'

Fore I can say anything he yanks me up on me feet an out into the corridor.

I aint even got the energy to fight. It's over. I can't do this any more.

I stumble, me knee gives way an I fall on the ground, yelpin with pain.

'Oy, get up you useless lump.' Garlic-breath kicks me in the side. I struggle to me knees but the sharp stabbin in me ribs makes me groan. 'I said get up!'

I cover me head with me hands waitin fer the next kick . . .

'You there!' The voice is sharp with command. 'Leave that boy alone.'

Garlic-breath stands to attention.

The man bends down next to me. 'Are you all right?' he asks, his voice gentle.

'Yes sir,' I mumble. He helps me up.

'Oh, don't call me sir! I'm not that old.' He smiles at me an I can see that even though he's big, he aint old at all. Maybe eighteen at a stretch, all wavy blond hair, blue eyes, an fancy clothes. The scent of lemons, fresh an sharp, surround him an fer some reason it calms me down.

He turns to stare at the guard. 'What is the meaning of this? Have you injured this child?'

'He was evading arrest sir,' Garlic-breath says but I can smell his nerves from here.

'Arrest for what? What crime has he committed?'

'Ummm . . . trespassing. Here in the castle.'

'Really?' The nobleman raises his eyebrow. 'You're arresting a servant of the castle for trespassing IN the castle?'

'He aint a servant!'

'I'm sorry? Isn't that a servant's uniform he's wearing?'

'Oh . . . yeah . . . but—'

'But nothing. Get out of my sight. If I see you in the castle again I'll have you in the stocks.'

The nobleman puts my arm round his shoulder an helps me down the corridor.

'Come on, into my study and I'll see to your leg.' He takes me into a big room filled to the brim with books an papers an maps, sits me down on an armchair an looks at me knee. 'So, have you won your dare then?'

'What? What dare?'

He pours water from a ewer onto a big white handkerchief he pulls from his pocket an wraps it round me knee. 'The kids are always doing it. Daring each other to sneak in and grab something from the castle, although they never went so far as disguising themselves as servants. It's a brilliant touch, I'm impressed. If you'd remembered to wear shoes I never would have guessed.'

I look down at me bare feet an curse meself fer a fool. The servants all wore wooden clogs, I'd been lucky no one else had noticed.

'So you knew I wasn't a servant all along?' I stare at the man in surprise. He winks at me.

'Of course. But it doesn't matter who you are, does it? The guards shouldn't be treating anyone like that,' he says matter of factly. 'There you are, how's that?'

I take a few limpin steps. 'It's good. Thanks.'

'My pleasure. Now, are you up for giving me a hand?'

'Course, if it wasn't fer you that guard'd have me guts fer garters.'

'Sounds painful!' He walks past me to a cupboard in the wall an pulls open the door. Inside is an enormous mildew-smellin hessian sack all tied up with string an lyin on the floor. 'It's too heavy for me but with your help I think we can manage it.'

'Blimey. What have you got in there?'

He bends down to pick up one end. 'Something very important and very secret. You can't tell anyone about it, do you promise?'

'Cross me heart.'

I pick up the other end an we half drag, half carry the heavy sack out of the cupboard.

'Iric?' There's a voice at the door.

'Oh fudge, he's here already,' he mutters, lookin nervous. 'Look, might be best if you stay in there for now, all right?' I aint got much choice though. Fore I can even ask why he pushes me gently back into the cupboard an shuts the door.

Luckily the door is made of wooden slats so plenty of light an air come in an if I bend down an peer through I can see everythin.

A man strides in carryin a big pile of paper, a hectic expression in his eyes. It's the same man I saw in the King's room less than an hour ago an now I'm proper grateful I'd been shoved in the cupboard cos I don't suppose he'd be happy to see me again.

'Uncle,' shouts me new friend. 'You can deny me no more. I have the proof you asked for!'

'What is going on? Why have you dragged me here?' I can see the family resemblance straight off but it's like the older man's been in the wash a few too many times an it's drained all the colour out of him. His hair aint as golden, his eyes aint as blue, an the moustache he's grown to hide his buck teeth sits like a pale white slug on his top lip. 'I really hope this isn't more of your nonsense, Iric.'

I gawp at the young man. Iric? Like in Prince Iric? Blimey. That means I've been chattin to the flamin heir to the throne an that man he was yellin at, that must be Lord Nash. I gulp.

'Come here Uncle, look at this.'

'Iric, I don't have time for this.' Lord Nash sighs with irritation an dumps his files onto the desk. 'Can't you see how busy I am? With your father sick everything falls to me, you know, I'm swamped with work and there's so much to organize, I've got meetings all day . . .'

Iric ignores him, marches over an opens the sack right at his uncle's feet. A thin, green, human-shaped body falls out of the sack on to the floor with a loud thump.

The stink of rottin seaweed bursts into the room an makes me gag an stumble backwards. Nash lets outta little squeal of disgust, turns white, an hunts his pockets till he finds a handkerchief which he holds over his mouth an nose.

The lifeless, broken thing leaks yellow blood on to the fine rug from a gapin wound in its belly, an its mottled skin is rippled with large moss-coloured scales. Its hands an feet have long, webbed fingers an toes an hard black nails on the end of em.

I've never seen one fore now but I know exactly what it is.

'There's your proof, Uncle. I told you the Boggers were planning something. You refused to listen but now, now I've brought you one of the foul creatures, you'll have to believe me.' Iric kicks at the dead Bogger, his voice low and furious.

'Stars above, Iric, have you gone mad?' Nash moves away from the ever-spreadin pool of blood, lookin like he's gonna puke any minute. The scent of fear an rage leaks past the menthol an camphor that infuses his skin.

'You left me no choice.'

'You're supposed to be a prince of the realm!'

'I am!' Iric insists, hands clenched. 'I'm trying to protect this kingdom as my father would want, but you won't let me. I am not a child, Uncle Nash, I'm sixteen now and I deserve to be heard.'

'I know you're upset about your father, Iric, we all are—but really, is that any reason to drag dead bodies into the castle?'

'But don't you see, Uncle? They're sending out spies. This one was found only a mile or so from the castle. All this time they've just been waiting for their chance and now, with my father out of the way they're planning their attack. You know he's the only one they've ever been scared of!'

Iric don't see it but from where I'm hidden I have a plain view of the look his uncle gives him fer that comment. It'd fair burn a hole through him, so filled with rage it is.

Nash shakes his head. 'For heaven's sake boy. There is NO threat. Nothing except the odd rumours and gossip and you should know better than to listen to it.'

'But this time . . .'

'No. No more, Iric. This pitiful specimen is not proof

of anything other than the poor creatures' continued miserable existence in the swamps. Just because a few of them cling to life out there and this one was unlucky enough to wander across the river means nothing. I won't have you spreading fear among the city with this madcap idea of yours!'

'But Uncle, you have to list—'

Nash squares his shoulders an lifts his chin. 'No. With your father sick I am the Regent. I am in charge and I want you to do as you're told for once.' He pauses, takes a breath. 'You will fulfil your duties as a prince and give up on this Bogger nonsense once and for all, do you hear me?'

I watch Iric struggle to accept his uncle's words but he nods finally. 'Now remove that creature and go and sit with your father like a proper son.' Lord Nash slams the door on his way out.

'I can't believe it.' Iric says, walkin over an openin the cupboard door so I can get out. 'He said he needed proof before he acted and now I've brought him proof and still he does nothing. What will it take for him to believe me? An army of Boggers knocking at the castle walls?'

He looks at me like he expects me to agree with him so I blurt out the first thing that comes into me head. 'Is that yer ma?'

'What?' I point at the portrait on the wall. 'Oh, yes it is.'

I dunno why I asked really cos the answer was obvious. 'Cor you're the spit of her aint ye?'

'That's what everyone says.'

'Must be nice fer yer pa that. Bein reminded of her all the time.'

'I don't think he sees it that way unfortunately.' Iric mutters. 'Anyway, what about you? Do your family live in the town?'

'Nah. I never knew me ma or pa.'

'Really? That's terrible. I'm sorry. My mother died when I was born so I know how hard it is.'

'It's funny though innit?'

'What?'

'How you can miss someone you never even met?'

Iric's eyes turn to the picture of his ma. 'Yes, yes it is.' He coughs an clears his throat. Straight away I tell meself I'm a fool. Talkin about Iric's dead ma while his pa lies dyin upstairs. I try an change the subject sharpish.

'So, ye gonna do what yer uncle says?'

Iric turns to look at me. 'No. I can't. There's a threat, I know there is.'

'But everyone said yer pa killed all the Boggers. Wiped em out completely.'

'No! Of course he didn't! I know it's what everyone thinks but it's not true. You've seen the proof of that!'

'An you reckon they're after revenge?'

'I know they are,' he mutters, his jaw tense an fixed with anger. The room goes silent. I aint sure what to say. Sounds to me like he's just usin this Bogger thing to cover up how upset he is about his pa. He looks so sad an broken, like a kicked puppy. Godric might not be the best king but I can see Iric loves him more an anythin.

'Y'know these Boggers aint as bad as I thought,' I say after a bit, pokin the dead creature with me toe. 'I mean, the way people talk about em I thought they'd be more scary, d'ya know what I mean?'

'Yes, they're scrawny little creatures aren't they? But they're much tougher than they look and they did very nearly beat us.' Iric bends down an starts wrappin the body back up in the sack. 'In fact they came close to wiping us all out. My uncle was overwhelmed by their sheer numbers and the way they fought, not like an army, not marching in file but swarming over everything, climbing the trees, the walls, hiding in lakes and streams, attacking at night with their blow darts and slingshots and spears. Poor Uncle Nash never really stood a chance. He was always far better with books than weapons, and when he got sick the army was nearly lost.'

'Luckily yer pa come an saved the day.'

'Yes, my father is a great soldier.' Iric smiles at me. 'And the people loved him so much for saving them that my grandfather made him king, even though he was the younger brother.'

'Didn't he mind? Yer uncle I mean?'

'Mind? About not being king?' Iric considers it fer a minute. 'No, I don't think so. He's always seemed perfectly happy as my father's right-hand man. Father's away so much he practically runs the place anyway!'

I'd be pretty narked I reckon but I suppose Iric knows his uncle better an me. Sides, Nash don't exactly seem up to it from the smell of potions an herbs surroundin him.

Iric ties up the sack an I move to help him lift it. The two of us carry it out of the library an take it outside to a big shed tucked away in the grounds.

'Anyway, I'll talk to him. I'll make him see. He can't ignore me for ever can he?' I think he'll probably try but I don't say it. 'You know you never told me your name?' Iric says, turnin round to look at me.

'Me? I'm Mold,' I tell him fore I can think of a lie.

'Well, thanks for your help, Mold.' He gives me a wide smile an the lemon smell gets stronger. It's risin from the core of him just like Begsy's did, I don't know why I can smell it right off with him. Maybe me sense of smell's gettin stronger or maybe Iric's just more open. Either way I know I can trust him, I'm sure I can. Perhaps I should explain about Aggy, he might even help me . . .

The faint scent of curdled milk slithers up me nose.

Me belly turns over.

It's him, it's the tattooed man, I'm sure of it, but there's another smell, even more familiar . . .

Mint! Strong an clear, just like the heart of only one person I know.

Begsy.

Chapter 11

I give Iric some excuse an run off, followin the trail, acid burnin a hole in me gut the whole time.

I've got a horrible suspicion Begsy's been plannin this all along, ever since I told him what happened. He'd sent me into the castle to sniff out the poison while he went an tracked down the tattooed man. He's tryin to keep me safe, like always—he thinks he can handle that toff hisself but it aint true. Begsy aint a match fer that flamin villain.

I run faster, followin the scent of mint, hopin I can warn him or sommink. The trail winds round the garden an through a large yew hedge but I have to stop cos the sudden burst of mint mixed with the iron tang of blood an death staggers me.

I force meself to keep goin through the hedge, hopin that somehow me nose is wrong, that maybe there's another reason fer that smell . . .

On the other side of the hedge is the most perfect rose-filled garden.

Perfect cept fer the dead body sprawled in the middle of it, gazin up at the sky with wide, sightless eyes.

Perfect cept fer the blood spreadin like a crimson pool over the white stone in the centre.

Perfect cept fer the villain standin over him, cleanin his silver knife on a clean handkerchief.

I can't move. Me chest is burnin an there's a scream in me throat that can't escape.

I'm too late.

Begsy is dead an gone an never comin back an I aint sure I can bear it.

'So good of you to join us and save me the trouble of tracking you down,' the tattooed toff says.

I ignore him. I move nearer so I can kneel down an close Begsy's eyes with a tremblin hand an whisper goodbye and I'm sorry an I love you an . . .

'Crying won't bring him back, boy.' I aint even noticed the tears streamin down me face like two small rivers till he says it. 'You two should never have come here. I warned you, I won't let anyone interfere in our plans. Especially not some scum from the Dregs.'

I should be scared probably. The way he's lookin at me an holdin that knife. But as I stare at his face an think of what he's done to me an those I love, rage burns up in me throat.

'You'll pay fer what you done,' I hiss. 'Whatever it takes you'll pay I swear it.' Fore he can even try an stop me I take off runnin, back through the yew hedge an round the side of the castle.

'Get back here you little runt!' he shouts after me but he must be mad if he reckons I'll stop. I run even faster, me feet barely touchin the ground. I pelt through a crowd of guards an jump over the low wall surroundin the castle. I pass the fancy houses. I don't look behind me but I can smell him. Smell the sour sweat on his skin an the rancid stink of fear. It makes me glad. I want him to be scared.

The runnin gets harder. Only rage keeps me going. Me legs are rubbery an I can hardly breathe. He's gainin on me I know he is, but I'm down to the second level now an the maze of shops.

I make a sudden turn into an alley, there's a sharp stingin on me arm but I keep goin. Another turn an another till I think I might faint. Or puke. Or both. I can't keep goin. I can't . . .

'Mold! In here.' Fergus appears from nowhere an yanks me into a buildin. He slams the door behind us an I collapse on the wooden floor pantin like a dog. Fergus peers through the window fer a minute then turns to smile at me.

'It's all right. He's gone straight past.'

I can't speak.

'Are you all right, Mold? Are ye hurt?'

I shake me head. Hurt don't come close. I might not

be injured but I'm bleedin all right. Bleedin on the inside an I don't think it'll ever stop.

Chapter 12

'Mold?' Fergus says after a bit. 'You really are bleeding y'know.'

I look up, eyes sore from cryin an see the fresh blood drippin down me arm from a thin cut. That must have been the scratch I felt. That scumbag must have thrown a knife after me an missed his target.

'It's nothin.'

'But what happened? Who was chasing ye?'

I take a deep breath, sit up, an wipe me face. I tell Fergus everythin. He should know what he's gettin into. He listens to me tale with wide eyes an I keep talkin, gettin it all out, every bit even though it hurts.

'. . . so if ye hadn't grabbed me he'd have probably killed me an all. To cover up his plans.'

'Cor, you was lucky I was here innit?' Fergus sniffs an wipes his nose. 'I was waiting outside the castle fer ages but then I got hungry an I thought I'd see if Olly the baker had any burnt bread I could have and then I saw ye come flying down Topps Alley with that toff behind ye. I cut down Blindman's Lane and ducked in here cos I knew it was empty like and . . .'

'Ye saved me life again,' I finish.

Fergus puffs his chest out. 'Well, we're partners aint we? That's what partners do.'

'It's dangerous though, bein partners with me. Are ye sure ye want to stay?'

'Course I do, Mold! I aint leavin ye. Not ever.'

I manage a quick smile fer him but I keep seein Begsy, lyin dead in a pool of blood an it rips me heart open every time.

'So what ye gonna do now, Mold?' Fergus asks.

'What Begsy would've wanted me to do.' I cram all the pain down deep inside me. Where it don't hurt no more. I have to. Fer Begsy. 'I'm gonna save Aggy an you're gonna help me.'

'I dunno, Mold,' Fergus says when I tell him what I need. 'It won't be easy. Big Sid runs the dungeons and he's not gonna let us in.'

'There must be a way, Fergus.' I chomp on some more of the burnt bread Fergus had managed to get hold of. 'It's important.'

Fergus thinks fer a bit while he stuffs the last half of his rye loaf into his gob an then wipes it with his sleeve.

'Well . . . we could ask Beetle,' he says at last.

'Who's Beetle?'

'He's one of the kids from the workhouse, he works fer Big Sid doing the night shift at the dungeons.'

'That sounds good, we could go there tonight then?'

'We could but . . . thing is Mold, Beetle aint quite right.'

'What does that mean?'

'Well, he's got a bit of a temper, see. Gets a bit violent. That's why they got rid of him at the workhouse. He kept beatin up all the people he didn't like and that included most of the wardens.'

'Oh.'

'So we can go and ask him if ye want but if he don't like ye Mold, he'll probably beat the tar out of ye.'

'Well, what sort of people does he like?' I ask, hopin he might have a fondness fer scrawny boys with big hooters.

'I dunno really but there aint very many of em.'

'Well, we'll have to try, we aint got much choice have we? I have to get to Aggy an we're runnin out of time.'

Beetle looks at me fer the longest while. I stand still like Fergus told me to but I'm impatient to get goin. We've already wasted hours in our abandoned house waitin fer it to get dark, then hid beside the dungeon entrance waitin fer the jailer to leave an fer Beetle to take over. Now we're finally standin in the cosy guard room, Beetle just keeps peerin at me like I'm some sort of bug he aint never seen before.

'Why's he got such a big nose?' he asks finally, his voice slow an thick as treacle.

'So he can smell things of course,' Fergus replies.

'Smell? What can he smell?' Beetle sneers at me.

'Anything,' Fergus says.

Beetle looks down at me, he towers over me by a foot or so an his arms an legs are as thick as tree trunks. His face is round an white like the moon with small dark eyes an fat blubbery lips.

'Anything?' he asks me, menace in his face.

'Aye,' I say, tryin not to let me knees tremble.

Beetle snatches up a jar from the shelf an thrusts it in me face. 'Go on then. What's in that?'

I twist the lid off an hold the jar up to me nose.

The stink of rotten fish guts an sheep fat slaps me in the face an I turn green an retch.

'What is it then, big nose?' Beetle has his thick arms crossed in front of him.

'Fish guts an sheep fat,' I tell him, chokin back the sick an twistin the lid back on sharpish.

'No it aint, you numpty. That there's the finest sea dragon milk.' He snatches the jar back off me. 'I bought it off a pedlar for twelve sovs to heal the ulcer on my foot.'

'Then yer a fool,' I tell him, still feelin queasy.

Beetle's hands snatch up the front of me tunic an lift me into the air.

'What did you call me?' he hisses, his furious face only inches from mine. 'You call me a fool when you don't know the difference between fish guts and sea dragon milk?'

I can see Fergus jumpin up an down behind him, panic all over his face an I wonder how close I am to gettin thumped.

'I know the difference between a real herbalist an a scammer!' I tell him.

'You're sayin that pedlar tricked me?' His grip gets even tighter an I'm strugglin fer breath.

'I'm sayin that it'd be near impossible fer anyone to milk a flamin sea dragon!' I choke out.

I can almost see the cogs turnin in his brain while he figures out what I mean an slowly the frown disappears from his face. Those flabby lips turn up in a smile an then a laugh an I see his gummy mouth with only a few black teeth still in it. Beetle puts me down, slaps me on the back hard enough to bruise, an keeps on laughin.

'I think he likes you,' Fergus whispers.

'Oh. Good.' I wait fer me heart to stop thunderin in me chest.

Beetle stops laughin at last an offers us a cup of tea. He might like me but I feel sorry fer the pedlar when Beetle catches up with him.

'Listen, Beetle,' Fergus says, drainin his tea in three big gulps. 'Mold needs to see one of yer prisoners, that's all right aint it?'

'Maybe. What one you want?'

'Aggy? The one in fer poisonin the King,' I tell him.

'All right then, but I don't want no trouble.'

'There won't be,' I promise. 'I just need to talk to her.'

'Good. Cos it'll be my job if anything happens to her. Lord Nash said he wants her kicking and screaming on the rope.'

I bite me lip an nod. Beetle lumbers up from his chair, grabs a bunch of keys from a hook, an opens the door.

I follow him down the dark stairs to the torchlit dungeons, the deep musty smell of despair risin up from below. Beetle plods along the damp an cobwebbed corridor, ignorin the pleas that come from the prisoners on either side, an stops at the last cell.

He unlocks the door an waves me in.

'Holler when you want out,' he tells me, lockin the door behind me.

The cell's small an cold with wet patches on the walls an just a thin sprinklin of straw on the floor. There's no bed, no chair, nothin cept a couple of buckets in the corner that I don't wanna think about too much. I watch Aggy drowsin restlessly against the wall an I'm shocked at the change only a few days has made in her. She's lost a fair bit of weight an now her skin sags in heavy folds round her face. Dark circles are smudged round her eyes, standin out against the paleness of her cheeks an her clothes are filthy, torn, an shiny with grease.

I bend down an take her hands in mine, the chill in em runs deep an it scares me. Aggy's too old to live like this an I'm worried she'll get sick.

Her eyes open, red-veined with tiredness but seein me there perks her up an she beams at me.

'Mold my love, I'm so pleased to see ya!' She pulls me in fer a hug an I hold her close, feelin fer the first time how frail she's got.

'Are you all right?'

'Course I am. Don't you worry about me.' She takes me face in her hands. 'How have you been managing?'

'Good.' I move out of her grasp fore she can see the lie there. I can't tell her about all the terrible stuff that's happened. I don't reckon she could cope. Not now. 'Everyone sends their love. They know you didn't do it.'

'I'm glad someone knows.'

'Course we do. You were set up weren't ye, by that flamin toff what come round the other day.'

Aggy sighs an sits back down on the straw. 'I'm sorry Mold. I shouldn't have trusted him but I never thought there was any harm in it, that tonic I made him was right popular years ago. The soldiers used to buy it cos it helped them go without sleep for a few days, kept them strong and healthy, stopped them getting sick in the swamps . . . I shoulda known he was a wrong un when he offered me a parvel for it.'

'It aint your fault Aggy. That toff was just usin you. Someone's paid him to get rid of the King an you're just the scapegoat.'

'I feel just awful though. His personal healer came down here this morning y'know. She wanted me to tell her what was in the poison, near begged me to tell her but what could I do? If I don't know, how can I tell her?' Aggy lets out a big sigh. 'Anyway my love, you shouldn't be here ye know. It's too dangerous in the city fer you.'

'Why? Cos I'm a Sniffler?'

'You know?' Her brown eyes fill up with tears that spill down her cheeks. 'Lawks I'm sorry Mold. I shoulda told you years ago but . . . well, I liked pretendin you were mine.'

'I am yours ye silly old bat.' I wrap me arms round her, huggin her close. 'I'll always be yours.'

'I knew you were special soon as I saw ye. My old gran used to live near the woods an she told me stories bout your people, they weren't treated kind if they were seen near the city, people thought they were bad luck or some nonsense.' She strokes me face with one hand. 'I took ye home with me to the Dregs cos I knew no one'd pry down there an I did my best to keep ye safe all these years . . .' Aggy breaks off, her voice twisted. 'And now look at the mess I've got us into. I'm a useless drunken old woman. Yer better off without me.'

'Now don't you talk like that!' I lift her chin an make her look me in the eyes. 'I'm fine an that other stuff don't matter except it means I can smell stuff an I made it to the King's chamber today an I sniffed his breath. I know what was in the poison an if you help me find the cure I reckon they'll let you go.'

Her eyes widen with surprise.

'You saw the King? Truly?' She sits up straight, lookin like the old Aggy again. 'Tell me love, how was he?'

'Not good. He looked pretty sick to me.'

'That poor man. I can't imagine who'd want to poison him.'

'Well, he aint been the best king lately, there are plenty of people who wish him gone. Whoever it was used henbane an dogweed.'

'Ooh, that's a nasty mixture sure enough but we can cure him quick as ye like. And you're right my love, if we can save him maybe they'll let me outta here, maybe we can go home? I'll do better this time, Mold, no more drinkin I swear it—'

'That aint it though,' I interrupt. 'There's gurdiskar root in it an all.'

Aggy's face falls. 'Are you sure, Mold?'

'Aye. Why?'

'I just can't understand how he's still alive if they've

used gurdiskar root. It works real fast and mixed with the other two . . . he should have been dead within minutes.'

'He's strong though, maybe that's saved him?'

'No one could survive that poison, don't matter how strong an fit you are.'

'But he has. He's alive, I saw him didn't I? But . . .' The reason comes to me in a flash. 'Your tonic! The bottle was in the King's room, that's what they used to frame ye. Maybe they mixed the poison with yer tonic?'

'My tonic? You could be right, Mold, it'd give him extra strength and work against the poison but I aint sure how long it can last.'

'Can you make more? Keep him alive longer?'

Aggy shakes her head. 'No pet, even if I had all the ingredients it takes three weeks fore it's any use.'

'Well, ye better tell me what the cure is then. Ye do know one, don't ye?'

'I do Mold, there's a cure fer any poison, even gurdiskar root but . . .' She pauses.

'What?'

'But the only place you'll find it is in . . .' She bites her lip. I wait. 'Oh Lord, Mold, it's in the Boggers' swamp.'

Chapter 13

'I'm sorry, Fergus, I gotta go,' I tell him later at the city gates.

'Let me come with ye, Mold,' he begs, almost hoppin with excitement. 'It might be dangerous out there, you'll need someone like me to help ye.'

'I'll be fine Fergus. I'll just get in, get the cure, an then I'm comin straight back.'

'But Mold . . .'

'Look, I gotta do this. I gotta save Aggy. An it's probly a good idea to get out of the city fer a while anyway, that rotten toff's gonna be after me hide fer sure.'

'Yeah, but you should let me help.' He sticks out his chin. 'I'm yer partner aint I?'

'I need you to do sommink even more important,' I tell him. 'Sommink I can't trust to anyone else.'

Fergus's eyes widen. 'What is it, Mold? You can trust me, you know that don't ye?'

'I do. That's why I need ye to stay here an look out fer Aggy.'

Fergus's shoulders slump. 'But Mold . . .'

'Listen, Fergus, Aggy's all I got. She took me in when I was a baby an raised me as her own, she's looked after me all me life an I owe it to her to help her now.' I swallow hard. 'I can't let nothin happen to her while I'm gone, promise me you'll check on her an take her a bit of food an stuff? Beetle'll let ye, won't he?'

'She must be real nice to take in a baby like that,' Fergus says, longin drippin from his words.

'She is, Fergus, an she's all the family I got now.'

'I'll look after her for ye Mold,' he says, his face determined. 'I promise I'll do a good job.'

I give him a quick hug an head out through the gates.

'Mold!' Fergus shouts after me. 'You will come back won't ye?'

'I promise,' I call back an he smiles an disappears into the crowds.

❧❀❧

Aggy didn't want me to do it of course. She made me swear not to go near the bogs.

'It's too dangerous,' she said. 'I'd rather hang than let you go squelching about in that place.'

Course, I'd rather risk the swamp than watch her hang, so here I am, sneakin onto a barge that's headin down the river towards Shillin. Fergus said it was the quickest way to the bogs an I aint got time to waste.

I dodge round the crates crowdin the dock an climb onto the flat deck of a large grey barge. There's a small space at the back in between a dozen oak barrels an I'm fairly sure no one'll see me here. I scrunch down, the yeasty smell of the beer in the barrels mixin with the faint salt tang in the wind.

I yawn an let the sounds of the sailors at their work fill me ears. This barge'll take supplies from Westenburg down the river to Shillin. That's where the big boats sail from, all across the Seven Isles, bringin back all the weird an wonderful stuff they have there, just like in Begsy's stories.

Sorrow stabs me. Knowin I'll never see him again. Never hear his voice or the clunk of his leg . . . I cram it back down again quick. I aint got time to mourn him now. I gotta focus on Aggy.

The barge moves away from the dock an the river current pulls it along at a fair pace makin the journey downstream quick an easy. On the return the sailors'll have to use long oars to drag em back up the river to Westenburg. Sommink I might get to see if I survive this trip to the bogs.

It won't be easy though. Aggy'd told me about some of the poisonous things you can find in the bogs when she was warnin me not to go.

'There's poisons in almost everythin my lamb; the julanti plants'll spit acid in yer face, the stripy Delen snake'll bite ya in the toe an you'll fall down dead two minutes later, the purple Narlo frog has poison in its skin, and don't forget the scarlet coral fish. She's a poison in her spines that'll paralyse you in ten seconds then slowly dissolve yer insides.' Sides all that there were strangler vines an giant lizards hidin in there. An if none of them got me I still had to find the rare Camberlinan orchid that grew in the mud an get it back to Westenburg in time to save the King. Easy.

I watch the riverbank pass me by, takin me further than I'd ever been, an it crosses me mind that I could just keep goin all the way to Shillin. I could get a job as a deckboy on a big sailin ship an set off to explore the world. Begsy said they were always lookin fer boys like me an it was a fine life, nothin but fresh air an adventure an freedom . . .

Except, I can't give up on Aggy can I? An I've made a promise to Fergus who's waitin fer me an then there's Iric an all who doesn't wanna lose his pa. There are too many people relyin on me to up an leave. An one person who still has to pay for what he's done.

Chapter 14

Me plan, if ye can call it that, is to stay right at the edge of the bog where it's safest, an if I keep in sight of the river behind me then chances are I won't get lost at least.

I wait till the barge is slippin across the shallow, swampy marshes an then lower meself off the side. Me feet squelch into the muddy ground an I push forward till I've left the river far behind.

The bog seems to stretch on for ever. Miles of mangrove an fig trees, their roots firmly planted in the deep mud, make a maze of firmish ground between the mulch. The air's warm an damp here an full of insects. They swarm round me, fillin me ears with a constant low dronin sound. Mixed with the rottin, sulphorous stink risin from the mud an the sickly sweet stench explodin from the plant life, an me head's soon throbbin.

I slap at the marsh flies feastin on me blood an keep walkin fer what seems like hours. The sun climbs higher in the sky, sweat drips into me eyes but there's no sign of any flamin orchid. I nearly step on a dull, brown snake though, an me heart jumps into me mouth when it hisses an rears at me.

Stumblin backwards I fall into the wet mulch an sommink sharp stabs me in the hand. Pain floods up me wrist an I curse loudly in the silent swamp. I scramble to me feet an look at the hole in me hand. It's swellin up an turnin red an I scan the ground fer any sign of what did it.

I can't see nothin in the boggy ground. The snake's vanished but the throbbin in me hand gets worse. I stagger over to a large tree an sit in its low branches while I examine me hand more carefully. I can just make out a small black thing stickin out of the hole an I use me fingernails to snag it an pull it out.

It's a verlinx thorn, vicious an painful but not deadly thank heaven. As soon as it's out the burnin disappears an though me hand's sore an swollen I'm relieved it's nothin worse. The longer I stay here lookin though, the more likely I am to run into sommink deadly an the less chance I have of gettin back to Westenburg fore the King dies.

I decide to try sommink different. I climb carefully up into the branches of the tallest mangrove tree around till I get a decent view. Maybe I can spot the flower from up here rather than searchin on the ground. Aggy said the orchid was tall, an with bright orange leaves an lilac flowers, so it should stand out against the relentless greens an browns that paint the swamp.

Course it would have been easiest if I knew what the damn flower smelt like, then I'd find it easy, but they're so rare Aggy aint ever been able to afford one even though they're one of the strongest antidotes around. She said if I crush the petals to a paste, mix it in with hot water, an let it steep fer a bit then the King'd be right as rain in a week or so. If only I could find it!

Me eyes search the ground, lookin fer the splash of colour that could save Aggy an the King, an when I finally see it, almost hidden in a patch of swamp thistles, I'm so excited I fall right out of the tree and land in a heap.

I reckon it's worth a few bruises though so I pick meself up an tramp through the mud towards the orchid. It takes me ages to reach it cos the ground gets increasingly boggy the further in I go but I finally make it to the thistle patch.

The flower's real delicate with rows of small lilac blooms an long orange leaves along the stem, it gives off a faint citrussy smell with a hint of honey. I squash the thistles down with a piece of wood to avoid bein stung an reach out fer the plant. The long stem pulls up easily, an even though it's just the petals I need, I decide to take the whole orchid back fer Aggy so I tuck it safely down me tunic. She'll like that I reckon.

All I have to do now is head back. I wish I'd brought

some water or sommink with me though cos I'm sweatin like mad in this heat an me mouth's drier an dust. I wipe me brow an look back to see how far it is to the river but all I see is swamp. The blue slash of water's nowhere to be seen.

I look all around but I can't see it anywhere. A prickle of fear runs down me spine. I've wandered too far away. I can't even smell the salt tang of the river cos the fetid stench of the bog's too strong.

It's all right though, I tell meself. If I turn around an start walkin I'm bound to find it again. I can't lose a whole river, can I?

I try an walk away but I can't move. I try again. Nothin. I look down an see that the mulchy mud is up to me knees. I've been standin still too long an now I'm stuck fast. I can feel the swamp tuggin at me feet, draggin me slowly deeper.

I search fer sommink to grab hold of so I can pull meself out but all I see are a pair of sulphurous yellow eyes floatin on the surface a few feet away. They lock on to mine, their long slitted pupils weighin me up. The harsh stench of hunger fills the air.

I can't breathe.

I hold meself still as a statue but it's no good.

The eyes move closer.

Someone screams.

I think it's me.

I flail me arms about tryin to get out of the mud fore that thing comes to get me but nothin happens cept I sink even deeper.

'Help!' I yell. 'Someone help me!'

The eyes are only an arm's length away.

I scream till me throat hurts but there's no one to hear me. No one to save me.

The eyes vanish under the mulch an I think me heart might explode with fear. Each beat sounds louder an louder, each one markin the last seconds of me life . . .

Pain rips through me leg, so bad I can't even scream, it sticks in me throat, chokin me, an then I'm tugged under the mud.

Chapter 15

Air rushes into me lungs. I flap an flounder like a fish on a hook. Agony burns through me leg. Hands clutch me calf an wrap it in sommink wet that eases the pain to just about bearable. I can hear words all around me but I can't understand any of em through the poundin in me ears.

I lie there shakin, tryin to work out why I'm not dead. I can hear a splashin an then a thump next to me. I open me eyes. A giant brown lizard, twice the length of me, with huge teeth an yellow slitted eyes, lies next to me on the flat raft. Two spears rise from its back an black blood leaks onto the wooden slats.

They've killed it.

The beast is dead an I've been saved.

The poundin in me heart slows down, the panic dies away an I let me eyes close. There are questions wormin their way into me brain but exhaustion an the constant throbbin in me leg stop me from payin attention. I just lie there, the gentle motion of the raft as it slips across the swamp an the low murmur of voices lulls me to sleep.

❧✿❧

I'm woken up by many arms liftin me off the raft an then dumpin me in a painful heap on the ground. The truth sinks in while I stare in shock at the camp around me.

Boggers.

Spite seein the dead body an hearin everythin Iric said about em still livin in the swamp I hadn't quite believed it. But now I've got no choice have I? They've saved me life an I'm here, surrounded by what looks like a thrivin village full of the scaly green creatures.

Their camp sits on a huge root system that surrounds a wide, round, bubblin swamp of blackness. A score of small mud huts are built round the edge while the low trees hold more huts made of wood an skins in their boughs. They blend into the scenery either way, makin em hard to see an easy to hide.

Hundreds of skinny Boggers, like the one I'd seen at the castle, scurry round the camp, all of em busy at some task or other; cookin, scrapin hides, sharpenin spears, fixin roofs, choppin fish. Even the little kids are kept busy with weavin baskets or grindin corn. There's a low hum of chatter while they work an a few voices sing what sounds like lullabies to the babies they carry in slings across their backs.

It's all so normal an peaceful I start to wonder if the pain's affectin me brain. I'd expected beasts. Creatures more like wild animals than humans, but they were just like us. Well, cept fer bein green an that.

Next to me, a group of fishermen start skinnin the great brown lizard an slicin its belly open to remove the guts. I try an wriggle away but the movement makes me leg worse so I have to lie there feelin sick.

The peace of the camp's suddenly broken by the arrival of a troop of fifty or so Bogger soldiers marchin out of the swamp an through the village, scatterin kids left an right.

These new Boggers are nothin like the villagers, they tower over em like giants. I reckon they must be near twice the size of a grown man an twice as heavy too. Their bodies are all thick corded muscle under heavy, armour-like scales. Huge black claws extend from their webbed hands an feet, an their teeth, when they snarl, are long an sharp.

The Bogger at the front dwarfs even these giants though, an his face is fierce with strange boar-like tusks piercin his jaw at either end an a great heavy brow shroudin eyes black as tar.

These are the creatures from me nightmares, the monsters I've imagined creepin into me window, but they aint supposed to be real. Questions flood me mind. Where have they come from? Did they crawl from the black, boilin mud fully formed an ready to kill? Are they the reason behind the rumours an whispers? Worst of all, are these monsters plannin to march on Westenburg? Cos if they are then Iric's in real trouble.

I keep watchin an a flap on one of the huts moves. An old, hunched, female Bogger emerges, wrapped in a mottled leather robe, skin gnarled an knotted with age, wispy bits of white hair pokin out of her head.

The troop of giant Boggers kneel down on the ground an bow their heads to her as if she was a goddess. Only the largest stays standin an clasps the old woman to his chest in a brief hug. There are muttered words between em an one of the fishermen creeps over an talks to em fer a minute. The wizened old hag turns an glares at me an a shiver runs up me spine.

Next thing I know they're both marchin over an standin round me, starin at me like I'm catch of the day or sommink. The old Bogger yanks me hair back an examines me, her putrid breath blastin into me face.

I cough an splutter an the old woman laughs an lets go of me hair.

'Hah, this is a fine catch! Bring him to my hut,' she says to the giant. He looks like he'd rather chuck me back in the swamp but he does as he's told, throws me over his massive shoulder an carries me into the old lady's hut.

He dumps me on the floor like a sack of spuds, ignores me scream of pain, an strides back out.

The old woman comes over an stares at me bleedin wound. She rips away me trouser leg an examines the bloody gash more closely. The next second she comes back with a clay bowl an pours the contents over me.

I scream like a stuck pig. It feels like acid clawin into me very bones. I try an crawl away from her but she holds me ankle an slaps some gungy paste over the teeth marks. A second later an the pain's gone. I relax an sigh.

'Better, yes?'

I nod. She helps me up an moves me onto a rough straw bed.

'No, I can't stay, I need to go.'

'Stupid boy. You must rest.' She holds me down an forces some poppy juice down me throat. Seconds later the world disappears.

Chapter 16

When I open me eyes again the wrinkled old woman's sittin by the bed. Her green scaly skin looks dry an rough as tree bark an she smells of dead fish an cabbage.

She notices I'm awake an holds a wooden cup to me mouth. I take a quick sniff. It's willowbark tea, good fer fever an pain but bitter as can be. Aggy always added a bit of honey to sweeten it but no such luck here. Me mouth puckers from the taste but I manage a few gulps.

'Tell me boy, who are you?'

'Umm, I'm Mold.'

'You're very lucky, Mold. I saved your leg.' She pulls back the fur blanket an peels away the poultice coverin the wound. I look down expectin to see the red-raw serrated gash from yesterday but only fresh pink flesh stares back at me with a thick red scar down the middle.

'How did you do that?' I gasp.

'I am Hexaba. I am a great healer. Rot from that murk

lizard infected your leg. If not for me you'd have lost it for sure.'

'I never seen nothin like it! It's like magic or sommink.' It's way beyond anythin Aggy could do, I know that much. Hexaba sniffs an pushes the poultice back in place.

'What are you doing out here in the swamps?'

I take another sip of tea while I try an work out what to say. 'Umm, I fell off my raft, washed up in the swamps, got lost . . .'

'You're lying,' she hisses, her pale blue eyes flashin.

'I never, I . . .' She stands up an waves the broken, sodden orchid I'd found in me face. I stop talkin.

'You were hunting the Camberlinan orchid. Why?'

'I need it, someone's been poisoned.'

'Poisoned with what?'

'G . . . gurdiskar root.'

The old witch slaps me round the face. 'No . . . gurdiskar root is deadly. There's no time for a cure.'

I throw the cup on the floor an put me hand up to me cheek. 'Well, this person's still alive!' I yell back. 'And they need the cure.'

'Still alive? Impossible,' she mutters.

'It aint impossible, it's true. Why would I be searchin the flamin swamps fer a cure if they're already dead?' I stop yellin an take a breath. 'Look, I need that orchid. Please let me go, let me take it back.'

'Pah. You think I'm a fool? You think we hear nothing

in the bogs? The King is the poisoned one! You're saying he still lives?'

I nod me head. The old woman growls under her breath. 'Why do you want to save this king, boy? Why?'

'Cos . . . he's the King.'

'Is he a good king?'

'Well, I dunno, not lately, but he is the King, so . . .'

'Pah. He's not your king, boy. You betray your own people by working for him.'

'Me own people?'

'The Dai Kurlin.'

I'm confused fer a minute then I figure out what she means. 'Ye mean Snifflers?'

'Pah, Bogger, Sniffler, these are the words of the Yellowhair. We're the mighty Skullensvar, you are the Dai Kurlin.'

Dai Kurlin? I was a Dai Kurlin. I stare at the old woman, wantin to hear more, an she obliges, gettin carried away in her anger.

'Our people were the first people, Pellegarno was our land until the Yellowhair come.'

I aint never heard any of this fore now. 'The Yellowhair? Where are they from? Why'd they come here?'

'They left their land of war and famine in big ships, they sailed for many months till they found a new place. Our place. They came and they never left. They stayed and stayed, took more land, then even more land—your people hid like animals, deep in the forests.' Hexaba gets up from the chair an starts pacin round the room. 'The Yellowhair bred like rabbits in their towns and cities, ruining the earth with their constant farming . . . and then they started coming to the bogs, trying to take our sacred land also but the Skullensvar are not weak like the Dai Kurlin. We rose up and went to war!'

Her face twists with grief an anger. 'We nearly won. We would have won if Godric had not come down upon us like a fury. Winning was not enough for him. He hunted us down like rats. Your people, my people. We were all nearly destroyed by their greed.' She points a bony finger at me. 'You are one of us boy. You should not work for them. You belong on our side.'

'Your side? But you lot killed all the Snifflers fer helpin Godric!'

'Bah, more lies! Godric may have forced your kind to find our villages but we never blamed them, they were victims just like us. In return for their help Godric betrayed them. Your people, your family, were sold to buy ships for this king that you're trying to save.' I stare at her wizened old face in shock.

'Sold?' I have to swallow hard against the lump in me throat. 'The Dai Kurlin were sold as slaves?' Was it true? Was that why Garlic-breath wanted me? To sell me as a slave?

'Yes, boy. Some of your people tried hiding but a few

soldiers were paid to hunt them down, the last few were caught and sold twelve years ago.'

'That's when me ma abandoned me in a bin,' I croak.

'Fool. Not abandoned. Your mother left you there to give you your freedom. You're the last Dai Kurlin in Pellegarno now. You belong with us, your gift should be ours. You owe us—after all, we saved your life, I saved your leg.'

'But . . .'

'But nothing. You will work for me now and be part of the new future of Pellegarno. My magnificent army will be ready to take its revenge any day now, they'll destroy the Yellowhair and the Skullensvar will rule all!'

I don't say nothin. I feel numb all over.

She smiles. 'I will send my apprentice Lireka with food. You eat then come work with me.' She leaves me shiverin in the bed, head spinnin, life turned upside down.

⁓⊙⊙⁓

I've hardly had a chance to think about me past an all the stuff I've heard what with everythin else that's happened an now it's all changed again. I lie in bed tryin to imagine a ma who'd loved me proper like. Who'd only left me behind to keep me safe from slavery. Not cos she didn't love me.

A warm feelin creeps into me belly. Knowin I aint been thrown away like a bit of rubbish heals a part of me I didn't even know was hurt.

The door flap moves an a little Bogger woman dressed in a lizardskin hide, this Lireka she mentioned I suppose, comes in carryin a tray. She looks at me carefully, her grey eyes wide, like there's a question there, but she don't say nothin, just dumps the tray on the table an scurries away like a nervous mouse. The smells from the food do nothin fer me appetite an I aint exactly eager to start work with Hexaba so I stay in bed an try an picture me ma.

Knowin she could be alive, that there could be others just like me out there somewhere was better an findin a purse full of parvels in the street. I wonder if I look like her or me pa, if they think of me at all. . .

An then I wonder where they are now. They could be livin on any of the Seven Isles but they'd be livin as slaves. Slaves might be beaten or chained or whipped. They might even be dead by now an I'd probably never know.

It hits me like a hammer. This family I been imaginin is lost to me. They've gone somewhere I'll never find em an they'll never be mine. An worst of all is knowin that the man I'm tryin to save is the reason fer it all. Cos of Godric's greed I've lost me true family an while tryin to find a cure fer him I've lost Begsy too!

Hexaba's words ring in me ears. I'm betrayin me own people by savin the King, by savin a man who aint just a bad king but has destroyed me whole tribe, an yet . . . an yet I know that if I don't save him, I'll lose Aggy.

Chapter 17

I'm pickin half heartedly at porridge that tastes like fish an some weird salty green seaweed bread when Lireka creeps back into the hut an scuttles over to me bed.

'Have you seen a boy?' she whispers. 'My boy? Near the city?'

'A Bogg—I mean, a Skullensvar boy?'

She nods, her eyes wide with hope. I get a flash of the dead Bogger in a bag in Iric's cupboard an swallow hard. I force meself to look at her an watch her face crumple at what she reads there.

'I'm sorry,' I tell her, squeezin her shoulder. 'He was caught near the castle.'

'I knew he was dead.' Tears run freely down her face but she makes no sound. 'I felt it in my heart but did not want to believe it.'

Guilt sits like a heavy stone in me stomach. I hadn't killed him but I hadn't given a thought fer his death neither an that was wrong.

When she looks at me again her eyes are hard as flint. 'She sent him out there. I knew it was too risky, I begged her not to send him but she doesn't care about us.'

'Who, Hexaba?'

Lireka nods 'She will bring doom on us all unless we can find a way to stop her.'

I'm about to ask her what she means when Lireka freezes suddenly an disappears under the door flap. Hexaba turns up a minute later an insists I follow her. I limp slowly behind her, a deep ache in me calf, but I'm amazed I can walk at all after yesterday.

The old crone leads me through the busy village, little Boggers scurryin out of her way like mice, all of em castin fearful eyes in her direction that make me wonder what they're so afraid of.

We end up at a big round hut tucked well away behind the others. The stink leakin from it makes me eyes water but I force meself to follow her in.

Like Aggy's cellar there are dried plants in the rafters, jars an bottles linin the walls, an a big table covered in knives an spoons. The familiar smells make me cough but it's the raw stench of fresh blood an rotten eggs that makes me guts cramp. It appears to be comin from a huge cauldron bubblin over the fireplace.

'This is a special place. For my most important work.'

'What? Potions an that?'

'Some. I'm the Skul Wican for our tribe. Healer, dreamer, leader. If not for me and my dream-magic our people would all be dead now. It was me, Hexaba, who hid the last of our kind from your bloodthirsty king.' She starts stirrin the pot over the flames. 'Me who bred new, stronger . . .'

The stink gets too bad. I can feel me stomach flip. I push out through the door an puke the disgustin breakfast all over the ground.

'Boy, what's wrong with you? Why are you sick like a dog?' Hexaba stands over me with a frown addin to the wrinkles on her face.

'It's the smell,' I tell her. 'It's too strong.'

'Ah, you foolish boy. It is your gift to smell but you must learn control. Come on, I don't have all day.' She drags me back into the hut an shuts the door.

'You don't want to smell this, no?'

I shake me head, me eyes still streamin.

'Then close the flaps, boy.'

'Flaps? What flamin flaps?' I cough.

'The flaps in your nose, boy! Skin flaps, Dai Kurlin can adjust them at will.'

I'm flummoxed. Flaps? In me nose? I dunno what she means. I can't feel nothin!

'Try!' Hexaba barks, yankin me closer to the cauldron where her noxious brew is bubblin. I can feel me belly rebellin.

I swallow down the bile an focus on me nose, I wriggle it, flare me nostrils but nothin happens.

'Come on! This is easy, the babies can do this.' She pushes me head down an holds it over the fire. 'There are remarkable things you can do with your nose boy, but first you must learn this!'

I struggle an fight against her iron grip. Me nose is burnin, belly crampin, head explodin an I can't do it, I won't smell it any more! A tight feelin runs across the inside of me nostrils an then there's nothin. I can't smell nothin!

I feel lost. Empty. Like I'm in a bubble or sommink.

Hexaba feels me relax an lets me go. 'See? You can do this.'

It feels weird. Like I've lost a part of me brain but at the same time there's a strange sense of pride cos I've mastered part of bein a Dai Kurlin.

'Now you can earn your keep, boy,' Hexaba says shovin a wrinkled mushroom at me. 'This is blood fungus. Very important to my work but very hard to find. They grow in the mud, deep down, but you can find them for me, yes?'

'I'll try,' I tell her but truth is I'm fibbin. If she lets me out of here I'm makin a break fer it. I have to. There aint much time left an whatever Godric's done in the past I won't let Aggy die. Not fer nothin.

A small Bogger pokes his head round the door flap an mutters sommink about 'a visitor'.

'Wait here, boy, I must deal with this.' Hexaba says, then narrows her eyes at me. 'I will send Lireka to take you into the swamp and keep you safe.'

I guess she aint stupid enough to let me out alone but it don't matter. I'll find another orchid an then I'll get away from Lireka. Hexaba might reckon I owe her sommink but that aint nothin to what I owe Aggy. Nothin.

Raised voices outside grab me attention an I peer out through the gap round the edge of the doorflap. I spy Hexaba, standin next to her's that enormous great Bogger with the tusks, an hidden behind him is someone else, someone with black snakeskin boots . . .

A shiver runs up me spine. It can't be. It don't make sense. But I have to know fer sure. I open up the flaps in me nostrils an take a deep breath . . . that familiar, hated, sour stench that I can't mistake slides up me nose. It is him. The tattooed man. But what's he doin here in the swamps? I push the door cover open an sneak towards em, ignorin the twinge in me leg an hidin round the trees till I get close enough.

'. . . it's true, it didn't work. He's still alive. I assume the poison you gave me is faulty.'

Hexaba snarls. The big Bogger stretches out an arm an grips the tattooed man round the neck, liftin him right off the floor. His cheeks puff out, turn red, then purple. His hands flutter at his belt, tryin to reach his knife but he's got no chance against this giant. I can't believe how much I want that big Bogger to keep right on squeezin.

'Enough, Bludengore,' Hexaba says just before he explodes. The giant Bogger loosens his grip an lets his victim slump to the ground. 'My poison kills in minutes. Minutes! You messed up, Marlow. You did something wrong.'

'Me?' he croaks, holdin his neck an glarin at Bludengore. 'I did exactly what you said. I bought some tonic from a useless old healer nobody would miss.' He ticks off the points on his fingers. 'I added your poison to it, I poured it into the King's wine glass, and he collapsed. If your poison didn't kill him it's hardly my fault.'

The breath catches in me throat an I curse meself fer a fool. The Boggers weren't just waitin fer their chance to strike, they were makin it happen!

Hexaba was behind the poison an the whole damned plot from the beginnin. All they'd needed was someone to give it to Godric an someone to blame an that's where Marlow an Aggy came into it.

'You oaf!' Hexaba shouts. 'You mixed poison with tonic? What tonic? What was in it?'

'I don't know! Some strengthening thing I think but that's hardly going to make a difference, is it?' He climbs back to his feet an straightens his tunic.

'Something worked. Something stopped my poison because the King is still alive and the plan is spoilt! It's all your fault!'

'Oh, calm down. The poison is working, just more slowly, the old fool will be dead any day now. In fact they're planning his funeral already.'

Hexaba sniffs. 'Good. We must be ready.'

'Yes, let's discuss your plans. I'll stay tonight and head back in the morning. Oh, and I have something for you in the boat, I'll fetch it now.' Marlow strides away, leavin Hexaba an the big Bogger mutterin.

A boat? Me heart beats faster. He said he had a boat? Course he couldn't get here by foot, could he? That meant there must be a channel nearby, an a way to get back to the river.

I have to find it. I have to get away from here right now cos if Marlow finds me here I'm dead.

Chapter 18

Marlow returns with a case full of wine. Hexaba rubs her hands together. 'A case of Godric's finest! Take it to my hut. We have much to talk about.'

I watch Marlow disappear inside an start sneakin in the direction he came from, hopin to find out where the boat an the channel is. Then all I have to do is find the orchid an escape. With a boat I should have enough time to get back. Enough time to save Aggy.

A giant hand crushes my shoulder. I freeze. Bludengore snarls at me, his lip curlin over his huge sharp teeth.

'Where are you going, worm?' The words rumble from his great chest.

'Umm...' My brain's stopped workin. His hand squeezes tighter.

'He's coming with me.' Lireka's voice interrupts. 'Hexaba is sending us out to find ingredients in the swamp.'

Bludengore glowers at me. 'Keep an eye on this one. Dai Kurlin cannot be trusted.'

'As you wish. Your mother is asking for you,' she says. Bludengore grunts, releases me finally, an marches off to Hexaba's hut.

'Hexaba is his ma?' I whisper. Lireka nods.

'Come, follow me and stay close.'

She scurries through the village an I do me best to keep up. She takes me past a small green bog on the outskirts that I hadn't seen before an waves at the Bogger women sittin cross-legged in its depths.

'Why are they all sittin in that bog?' I ask her.

'Come, you will see.' She leads me closer. 'Milla, the boy wishes to learn our ways.' One of the women gets up an shows me the mottled green an brown egg, about the size of a melon, that she was sittin on. I think me jaw drops open but Lireka an the woman laugh. It sounds like any other laugh an I find meself smilin back. Soon other women come an join us, one of em shows me a tiny green baby still wet from hatchin. It stares at me with wide blue eyes, its webbed fingers reach towards me an grab hold of me nose.

The baby's ma chuckles an gently eases its tiny hand away. Lireka waves me to follow her an we leave the nestin mas an their babies behind an head away from the village an out into the bogs.

Chapter 19

It's easy enough to sneak off. I've been followin Lireka good as gold fer a long while, just waitin fer a sniff of the orchid. She don't even notice when I let her get further an further ahead an when the first whiff of honey slithers up me nose I head off after it.

It aint quite the same smell as last time, there's a sour note to it, but it's the only thing that's come close an I'm runnin out of time. I follow the scent trail, usin me nose flaps to block out all the other pongs an keepin a wary eye out fer any lizards.

Sweetness overwhelms me, sickly sweet . . . not the orchid . . . sommink else . . .

I'm yanked off the ground by sommink that's wrapped itself round me throat, squeezin so tight I can't breathe. I try an get me fingers under it but it's just too tight an I can feel me eyes bulgin, me legs kick helplessly . . .

There's a flash of silver, the pressure vanishes, an I fall back down to the ground in a heap.

I draw deep lungfuls of air into me chest an tug the green vine from me throat an throw it far away.

Lireka stands over me, a wicked-lookin silver blade in her hand. 'Strangler vines,' she says. 'You were lucky I was following you. They strangle their victims then drag them into their root bulb where they're dissolved in acid and slowly absorbed.'

I gulp. 'You were followin me? All this time?'

'Yes.'

Course she was. I was daft to think I could escape her, that I could make it out of the swamp alive. Hot angry tears slide down me face an I wipe em away with me sleeve.

'Is this what you were searching for?' She takes a leather pouch from her belt an hands it to me.

I open it up an see the orchid inside. It's a bit battered an half its petals cling to the inside of the pouch, but right now it's the most beautiful thing I've ever seen.

'Aye. This is exactly what I was lookin fer.'

'Because you wish to save the King?'

I nod. 'But only cos savin him's the only way to save my Aggy.' I scramble to me feet so I can explain properly. 'If he dies they'll hang her an she's all I got.'

'Then you must take it now and go.'

'You'd let me go an save him? After everythin he's done?'

Lireka sighs an shakes her head. 'Perhaps if we help save

his life he will understand that most of us do not want another war. That desire is all Hexaba and Bludengore. You must tell him the true Skullensvar send him this cure as a token of peace.'

'I'll tell him. I'll explain everythin I promise.'

'You are a brave boy to come here. This Aggy is lucky to have you.' I know she's thinkin bout her son. Sadness seeps from her pores, sweet rose tinged with sage. I can't help it, I reach out an hug her, real careful. She's frozen fer a moment an then her arms move an she squeezes me back real hard.

We stay like that fer a minute then she releases me an clears her throat. 'So, it is nearly dusk, I will take you to where we keep the boats. You will take one and leave this place. Hexaba will be too drunk on Marlow's wine to notice anything tonight. When she wakes and finds you gone I'll tell her you must have escaped during the night.'

'Won't you get into trouble?'

'Perhaps. She won't do me much harm though, I'm far too useful for that.'

We wind our way back through the swamps towards the channel. The village is less than a hundred yards away so we move slow an quiet.

When I sniff out a clutch of the metallic-smellin blood fungus under a big mangrove tree an dig down deep in the mud to find em, Lireka shakes her head an frowns.

'If you give her these she might not be so mad at you,' I hiss. 'Please. I don't want ye to get into trouble over me.'

Lireka huffs but takes two an puts em in her pouch. 'There is only dark magic that can be done with these.' She stomps the rest of the fungus into mush. 'We must be careful how much power we give her, she is quite mad with her lust for revenge.'

Over by the boats Lireka takes her leave an I can hardly find the words to thank her for her kindness.

'Your people loved this land, Mold, they desired only peace. Perhaps somehow you can find a way to bring it?' She's gone fore I can say anythin, meltin back into the swamp like a ghost.

'I'll try,' I whisper. 'I promise I'll try.'

Chapter 20

Tied up on the small stream are a couple of rafts like the one that rescued me from the murk lizard and one barge with a deck an a hold an a great big paddle on the back. That must be Marlow's.

Obviously that's the one I take. I wish I could see his face when he sees it's gone an works out he's gotta use a raft to get back up the river.

I climb on board, the pouch with the orchid is hangin round me neck an tucked under me tunic. Lireka said cos it's made from murk lizard skin it's waterproof, but I told her I weren't plannin on doin any swimmin.

I have a quick search to see if there's any food or water on board cos me belly's empty as a beggar's purse, but there's nothin much on deck an the catch to open the hold is stuck fast. I wriggle it harder but it slips out of me fingers an I bash me hand which makes me swear.

I give up an untie the moorin rope an grab hold of the paddle. I'm about to start off when I hear this weird knockin sound. I keep listenin. It's comin from the hold.

I give the catch a kick an it opens with a click. I pull the small hatch up an Fergus's head pops out like a jack-in-the-box.

'Fergus? What the flamin heck are you doin in there?'

'Mold! Am I glad to see ya!' Fergus beams at me, green eyes shinin in the gloom. 'I was visiting Aggy at the jail when I saw that toff who was chasin ye before an I thought I'd follow him like an see if I could find out who he was workin for. I sneaked on this boat an hid in the hold when he weren't looking but then the catch fell down an I couldn't get out an I been stuck here fer ages!'

I should be cross but truth is I'm sorta glad to see him. I grab his hand an help pull him out.

'I'm sorry, Mold. I know ye wanted me to stay with Aggy.'

'Aye, well you're just lucky it was me what found you an not Marlow. Now I'm takin this boat an headin home, are you comin with or do ye fancy stayin?'

'No fear, Mold, it smells rotten here. How can ye stand it?'

'It's me noseflaps. I can close em see an shut out all the pongs. That's how come I never smelled ye. Anyway, sit down, we've gotta go.'

I push the paddle into the water an we set off by moonlight. The channel's narrow but gets wider the further we go. Fergus reckons it's only half an hour till we get to the river, but rowin back against the current to Westenburg'll be hard work, so it's maybe two or three hours till we make it back.

Fergus's voice, the hummin of midges an the soft slap of the paddle in the water are the only sounds in the swamp. We glide along the channel, the cool night air a welcome relief from the stiflin heat, an I fill Fergus in on what I've learnt.

'They're gonna attack? A giant Bogger army? But that's terrible, Mold. Where've they even come from?'

'I dunno Fergus, I'm too tired to think any more. I just wanna get back, give Godric the cure, get Aggy out of jail, an tell Iric it's worse an he thought.'

'Do you reckon we'll be heroes, Mold? If we save the King and warn em bout the Boggers? I'd like that. Maybe Godric'll give us medals or something?'

'You'll have to have a proper wash first if ye wanna meet the King,' I tease him.

'I do wash! Soggy Joe hoses us all down when we finish work fore he lets us back in the barn.'

'That aint washin. Ye need a nice big tub first like the one the King's got, fill it up with hot water, add some soap to make ye smell nice.'

Fergus wrinkles his nose. 'Cor I don't wanna smell like a girl, Mold. Anyway, I don't smell that bad, do I?'

I don't answer though, cos I can see the river ahead, like a silver ribbon in the black, an all I can think about is escapin this foul place once an fer all. I start paddlin faster.

'We're nearly there Fergus. Look.'

The river's only yards ahead now. I can feel the current tuggin at our boat, pullin us closer an closer till it's right there in front of us.

Fergus gets so excited he practically runs to the front of the boat, which rocks wildly under his weight.

'Careful,' I tell him.

'Blimey, I nearly had a bath then after all!'

We're both laughin when the boat tips suddenly, violently, an throws us both into the water.

I fight me way up to the surface coughin an splutterin.

'Fergus? Fergus!' I shout but there's no sign of him anywhere. I kick me legs, tryin to stay afloat but panic's settin in. 'Fergus!'

Flamin heck where is he? I spin round wildly an then finally, just behind me I see movement. I kick towards him, waitin to see his little freckly face emerge.

But it aint Fergus I see. Instead the hideous tusked face of Bludengore rises out of the water, teeth barred in a grimace.

'I knew Dai Kurlin cannot be trusted! Your people betrayed mine before and now you would do it again, returning home to warn them of our plans.' He reaches out a massive arm towards me.

Fear seizes me an I kick wildly away from his grasp

but it's no good, his great bulk bears down on me an his fingers clamp round me wrist like a vice, draggin me towards him.

'Gerrof!' I shout but Bludengore only yanks me harder an all me strugglin comes to nothin against his enormous strength.

His other hand grabs me round the neck, liftin me up into the air an chokin the breath from me, fore plungin me back down into the depths of the river.

Water rushes into me nose an mouth while I fight an claw at the hand that holds me fast. I can see his face above me, those pitiless black eyes barely flicker as me limbs get heavier an heavier an me lungs burn an crackle . . .

The weight holdin me down disappears all of a sudden an I burst out of the water, gaspin an chokin an tryin to figure out what happened. I gawp at the sight of Fergus clamped to Bludengore's back, his fingers jabbin at his eyes.

'Go Mold!' he yells. 'Quick.'

'Fergus?' I try an move towards him but I've no energy left an the current tugs at me hard, yankin me backwards.

'Fergus!' I scream, throat burnin, but I can't fight the river an it drags me away from the swamp, into its cold, relentless grasp.

Fergus, still attached to the giant, smiles at me as I'm swept away, rippin me heart out as I go.

Chapter 21

The sailor who drags me out of the river with a bilgehook dumps me on his deck like an overgrown fish. I puke me guts an half the river up on the sun-bleached wood an lie there shiverin an wishin I was dead.

One of the crew brings me a blanket an some water an forces me to sit in the hold with the oarsmen. It's warm an dry down here but I can't seem to stop tremblin as I watch the sailors pull at their huge wooden oars, draggin the barge up the river to Westenburg. The slow steady beat of a drummer keeps time for em but with each pound I see Fergus again. His small skinny body wrapped round that ferocious giant just to save me . . . his stupid gappy smile even while I left him there, all alone, with a murderous Bogger.

Pain stabs in me belly.

I shoulda gone back.

I'd tried of course but the current was too strong an the freezin water robbed me of any strength I might have found an in the end it was all I could do to stop meself from drownin as I drifted down towards Shillin but . . . I should have tried harder. Better still, I should never have involved Fergus in all this in the first place.

He thought it was all some big adventure but I knew it was dangerous. Too dangerous fer a little squirt like him. But I hadn't cared about that, had I? An now he was dead. Killed by that evil Bludengore.

My guess is he was watchin fer Lireka an when she come back alone he'd set out after us, hidden like a murk lizard in the water where I couldn't smell him, an then tipped our boat just fore we could escape.

If it hadn't been fer Fergus I'd be dead now. But he'd sacrificed hisself fer me an now I have to make sure it was worth it.

I have to save Godric.

Even if there's a little voice sayin that maybe he deserves to die fer the wrong he's done to the Skullensvar an the Dai Kurlin an lately even his own people.

I have to save him anyway, an not cos Lireka wants me to or cos Westenburg needs him or even cos Iric loves him. The only reason big enough or strong enough fer me to save that louse now is Aggy.

I can't lose her. I've lost Begsy an now Fergus is gone so she's all I've got left in the world. There aint nothin I won't do to get her back. Nothin.

Chapter 22

I nearly make it. It's dark when I get to the castle an the servants are half asleep so it's easy to grab a tray an an apron an wander through the halls like I belong there. I make it all the way to the King's door fore I get stopped.

'No one's allowed in. New orders,' the young, beefy guard says, not even lookin up.

'But . . . I been sent to clear up,' I lie.

'Tough. The Prince is in there with his father and doesn't want to be disturbed.'

'Look,' I say. 'Prince Iric knows me. He'll see me, just tell him it's Mold.'

The guard raises one eyebrow at me. 'Yeah, course he does.'

'He does, honest.'

'Look, run back to the kitchen and stop bothering me. Orders is orders.'

'But this is important! Just tell him, please.'

The guard steps towards me an jabs his finger into me chest. 'I said get lost, kid!'

'No. I've gotta see Iric.' I try an move past him to the door but he grabs me by the shoulder an starts marchin me away. 'No!' I yell, fightin hard as I can. 'IRIC!' I bellow.

'Oy! Shut your cakehole, you!' The guard puts his hand over me mouth to shut me up so I bite him hard. 'Owwwwwww!'

The door opens. The Prince stands there, face pale, eyes red, an stares at us in confusion.

'What's going on, Alnor?'

'Um, I'm sorry Your Highness. I was just taking this . . .'

I push Alnor's hand away. 'Iric,' I wave. 'It's me, Mold! Remember? I need to talk to you, it's important.'

'Mold?' Fer a minute I think he's forgotten all about me but then his eyes clear an he gives me a quick smile. 'It's all right Alnor. You can release him, it's fine.'

'Yes sir.' The King's guard lets me go.

'Told ye he knows me,' I mutter. Alnor pokes his tongue out at me an I grin back at him.

'What's so important then?' Iric asks.

'Can I come in? Tell ye in private?'

Iric nods. 'Alnor, take your break now. I'll be fine.' He waves me in, shuttin the door behind us. I take a quick glance at the King, his chest barely risin as he breathes an his face all white an sweaty. Looks like I've made it just in time. The King won't last the night, I'm sure of it.

'Go on then, Mold. What's so urgent?'

I swallow hard an start with my confession. 'That day, that day we met I wasn't here to steal buns from the kitchen. I come here to sniff the King's breath an find out what was in the poison.'

'What?' Iric stares at me like I've grown another head.

'I'm a Dai Kurlin.' He still looks confused. 'A Sniffler?' Understandin dawns in his eyes. 'Anyway, I found out what was in the poison an then I found out the cure an I went lookin fer it . . . in the swamp.'

'But why? Why did you want to cure my father in the first place?'

I take a deep swallow. 'Cos of Aggy. Cos I knew she never done it an if I was gonna save her from hangin I had to save yer pa first.'

I blurt out the rest of the story. I tell him how Aggy got set up an everythin.

'But why would this man want to poison my father?'

'Cos he was paid to . . . by the Boggers.'

Iric's jaw falls open. 'What? What do you mean?'

'I found the cure in the swamps, Iric, but I got caught by the Boggers an taken to their camp. It was their leader Hexaba who made the poison an paid Marlow to give it to yer pa. Her an her son Bludengore want him dead just like you said, so they can attack, an they have a great army of monsters all ready to fight an take their revenge.'

Iric strides round the room like a caged bear. 'The Boggers? All along it was the Boggers and they're planning to attack? They have an army?'

'Aye. So you have to give yer pa the cure, you have to save him.'

'And you have this cure, Mold?' Iric stares at me, hope sparkin in his eyes.

I nod slowly an take the orchid out from the pouch under me tunic. 'Lireka gave it to me an she helped me escape. She says most of the tribe don't want war, only peace. It's Hexaba an her son behind this plot. You have to make sure yer pa knows that.'

'I will, Mold. I promise.' He means it, I know he does. His hand reaches fer the orchid. I take a step back.

'I aint sure he deserves it though.'

'What? Why not?'

'Cos this flower cost me, Iric, it cost me dear. Two of me best friends were killed so I could find this orchid an bring it back to you.' I gulp hard, tryin to stop the tears from fallin down me face.

'I'm sorry—' Iric says but I talk over him, needin to get it all out.

'An then I find out that the very man I was tryin to save, your pa, sold the Snifflers as slaves . . .'

'Mold, no, the Boggers killed the Snifflers.'

'No they didn't! Yer pa sold em an they were all sent

to the other Isles to live in chains just so he'd be rich enough to buy his flamin ships.'

Iric's face is pale, he shakes his head. 'No . . . he wouldn't, he didn't . . .'

'He did!' I shout, anger bubblin in me guts. 'He's the reason I never knew me parents. They left me here to save me from slavery an now I'll never ever find em. They could be dead, all of em. Cos of him.'

'Mold . . . I'm sorry.' Iric's sky-blue eyes are wide. 'I had no idea of any of this. I swear it.'

'I aint even sure yer pa deserves to be king any more after the things he's done.'

Iric swallows his denials. 'Please, Mold. Give us a chance to make things right?'

I look down at the orchid in me hand. I'm so tempted to throw it in the fire but . . . the look on Iric's face stops me. I hold out me arm an give him the flower.

'You have to crush the petals an steep em in boilin water, then he has to drink it.'

'Thank you, Mold. Thank you.' Iric takes the orchid. 'I will ensure Aggy is released as soon as possible and then I promise to try and make it right somehow. All of it. You have my word.'

I nod. I may not trust Godric but his son's another matter. 'Best get that brewin then. He aint got long.'

Iric can't wait fer a servant an heads off to the kitchen to fetch a kettle of water himself so we can steep the petals. I sink into the big leather armchair feelin limp as a dishrag. Too much has happened an I hardly know which way's up any more. Part of me's happy, part of me's grievin an the only thing I know fer sure is that I'd like to sleep fer a week.

A massive yawn ripples through me an I stretch out me arms wide as can be.

CRASH!

I jump up an stare in horror at the smashed vase on the floor. I kneel down an try an pick up all the pieces, hopin it aint some priceless heirloom or sommink. I have to squeeze right behind the chair to reach some bits an when I look back up the door's opened an Lord Nash has walked in.

I almost say sommink to let him know I'm there. I open me mouth an everythin but then I panic an decide to just hide behind the chair till he's gone.

'Hello Godric. The healers tell me you haven't long left so I thought I should pay my last respects.' He clears his throat.

I cringe behind me hands, eavesdroppin on Nash's private farewell to his brother aint good but I can hardly pop up now, can I?

'You have suffered haven't you, dear brother? Wasting away for days and days, I don't think I can watch it any longer. I shall put you out of your misery.' I peek over the side of the chair an watch him pick up a pillow an lower it over his brother's face.

'Wait!' I leap out from behind the chair. 'Don't! I've found a cure, Godric's gonna be all right.'

Nash stares at me in shock but he removes the pillow. 'What? A cure?'

'Aye, I found it in the swamps.'

'Well, aren't you a clever boy.' The sarcasm aint exactly lost on me an a sick feelin of dread starts churnin in me belly. Then I notice the birthmark on his wrist is clover-shaped . . .

There's a clatter at the door an Marlow bursts in. He looks terrible, pale an sweaty with dark circles under his eyes. Just like Aggy'd look the day after there was a party in the Dregs with free booze.

'My Lord,' he gasps. 'We might have a problem.' An then he sees me standin there an his jaw drops open. 'How did you get in here? What have you done?'

'You know this lad?' Nash's voice is sharp an angry, full of power an control. Not like I've ever heard it before.

'It's the healer's brat, my Lord.'

'The healer's brat?' He looks confused fer a second an then understandin dawns across his face. 'The one from the Dregs? But you said you'd got rid of all the witnesses!'

His words confirm me very worst thoughts. Nash was in on it all. The whole plot. Marlow worked fer him and the Boggers. I remember now he was at the King's door, he was probably there to see Nash but I never suspected fer a minute, there'd been no scent of betrayal from the King's brother, nothin.

'I did! I even burned their stinking hovel down and barred the door but somehow he got out. He's been trying to find a way to save the old biddy. He came looking for me here and I just found out he was in the bogs—'

'You knew he was alive? And you've done nothing about it? What's the point of making you chief of my intelligence network if you can't even kill a little wart like him?'

Marlow turns even paler. 'I apologize, my Lord, but really he's no threat. No one would believe the word of a Dregger brat.'

'And yet he's here in the King's bedroom with a cure apparently.'

'We can put paid to his plans right now,' Marlow says quickly. 'We kill him and the King and let that be the end of it.'

'Yes. We shall have an end to it.' Nash smiles at me, the mask of noble lord gone from his face an in its place the vicious, twisted sneer of a man who'd betrayed not just his brother but his people too.

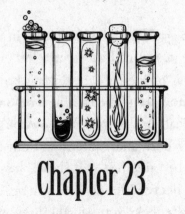

Chapter 23

Nash strolls towards me. I shrink back, away from him. Away from the putrid smell that's exploded into the room. A stink like dead rats stuffed in a box an hidden under the floorboards fer years.

'You look familiar,' Nash says, peerin into me face. 'Something about the nose . . .'

'Hexaba said he was a Dai something,' Marlow tells him. 'Said he was in the swamps sniffing out a cure to the poison with that great conk of his.'

'Really? A Dai Kurlin? How fascinating. I thought I'd got rid of the last of you freaks years ago.'

'You?' I ask. 'You were the one who sold off the Dai Kurlin?'

'Yes, my brother wanted coin for his ships and selling off that misbegotten tribe was the easiest way to get it. Godric never cared where the coin came from for his schemes, as long as it was there. He signed the papers quick enough.'

'How could you? This was their land in the first place, fore you stole it. You had no right sellin em into slavery an all!'

'Don't be a fool, boy. The right is always with the ruler, never forget that. And very soon I will be the ruler here and I won't have my plans spoilt by you or anyone. The kingdom will be mine just as it should have been, just as my birthright decreed.'

'But you were sick, you had the lung rot, how could you rule?'

'That's what they said, said it was for my own good but it was theft pure and simple. I was well again after a few months but all my life people have treated me as if I were sick, sick and weak, yet I'm the one who's been running the country, doing all the boring work Godric can't be bothered to do!'

'I reckon you are sick. Sick in the head.'

Nash backhands me across the face, the force of his blow splittin me lip an knockin me backwards.

'How dare you!' he roars. I roll over, moanin an clutchin me face, blood pourin into me hands. 'Godric stole my glory and my crown and I will be avenged.'

I push meself to me knees. 'How? By killin yer own brother an betrayin us all to Bludengore an his monsters?'

'Bludengore works for me! Marlow came to me with Hexaba's plan and I knew my chance had come at last.

Marlow has negotiated with them on my behalf and we have agreed I will be king and Bludengore will be my war leader. I shall send him and his army to the other Isles and we will conquer them all until I am ruler of an empire too glorious for you to even imagine!' I can almost see the veins poppin in his eyes.

'You've never even met Hexaba an Bludengore? Then you've no idea what you've done.' I make it back to me feet but me head is spinnin. 'They're plannin to attack ye know. Did yer little toady tell ye that?'

'You're starting to bore me.' Nash glances over at Marlow, a tiny seed of doubt in his eyes. 'Take him away. I'll finish my brother off, I'm going to enjoy it after so many years of waiting.' He steps over to the bed.

'Uncle?' Iric slams the door shut behind him. He bangs the tray holding a tin kettle an a goblet down onto the sideboard. White hot fury blazes from his eyes. 'It was you all along? Poisoning your own brother? Working with the Boggers? How could you?'

'Quite easily really. I've had enough of playing second fiddle to my glorious brother.' He points at Iric. 'It's my turn now and you will not stop me.'

'But . . .'

Godric coughs, his weakened body spasming up an down, distractin Iric from his argument. He grabs the goblet an rushes over to the bed.

'Drink this, Father. It will help.' He holds the gold cup

to Godric's mouth. I will Iric to get the potion down him fast as he can . . .

'No you don't!' Marlow shouts, knockin the cup from Iric's hands an spillin the potion all over the bedclothes. 'There'll be no cure for Godric.'

'Curse you!' Iric bellows, flyin at Marlow fists first. He gets in a few good hits but Marlow fights back, windin Iric with a sharp jab to the ribs an then smashin him in the face, drivin Iric down to the floor.

'Enough,' Nash orders. 'There's no need for us to dirty our hands, I've got a better plan. Come Marlow, it's time for us to leave.'

'You can run, Nash, but you'll never get away with this!' Iric hisses, his nose drippin blood onto the rug.

'I think you'll find I'll do more than get away with it because everyone will believe it was you who poisoned the King.'

'What? You can't mean . . .'

'Oh, but I do. The Prince and the poisoner's boy in league to kill the King, it's too perfect.' He shakes his head slowly, an evil glint in his eye. 'And all I have to do is lock the door. Your father won't last the night and in the morning you'll be discovered together . . .'

Iric turns pale. 'No one will believe it.'

'Well, they believed Godric was the one putting up the taxes, cutting the wages, and refusing to buy food for the poor when it's been me all along.'

'Well they won't believe this! The people know me.'

'How could they not believe it, Iric? My network of spies will whisper in their ears. The people love me now, they think I care about them! I was going to ensure you had a terrible accident within the year but now I'll just have you hanged as a traitor.'

I gulp. It could work. His plan made some sorta dastardly sense.

Iric's fists clench with rage but Marlow takes a long steel blade from his belt an points it at us both. Nash heads to the door. 'Good night, nephew. Enjoy your last few hours with your father.'

'Yer a fool,' I tell Nash as he opens the door. 'Bludengore an Hexaba hate all the Yellowhair. They're just usin ye to get rid of Godric so they'll be free to attack.'

Lord Nash smiles thinly. 'I forgot one thing, Marlow. Head down to the dungeons and finish off that old healer will you? We've no more use for her now.'

The door slams shut an a key turns in the lock.

Chapter 24

I kick the door. It don't help an it ruddy hurts but I can't help it.

'That's it then,' Iric says. 'It's all over.'

I turn me head an look at the blood-soaked prince, slumped on the floor near his pa who wheezes with each an every breath. How had it all gone so wrong, so quick?

'I'm sorry, Iric. I shoulda known, I shoulda smelled it!' I reckon the menthol an camphor he wore must have helped mask his true scent but I still felt like an idiot.

'You? What about me? He's my uncle for pity's sake! I can't believe he pretended for all these years. I can't believe we missed the fact that he hated us all this time!'

'He must have been a master at pretendin, at hidin how he felt.'

I can hear words an footsteps from outside. I peek through the gap in the door. Two blue-jacketed guards stand there, to attention. Swords hangin at their hips.

'Nash has put guards outside. Can't you get em to open the door?'

'I doubt it.'

'But you're the Prince, surely the guards'll have to listen to ye?'

Iric sighs. 'No, Nash is the Regent. The Royal Guard have to listen to him. The only one who can countermand him is my father and . . .' Iric's voice breaks. 'I was so close to giving him the cure and now look, it's spilled all over the floor and there's not one petal left. I used them all.'

I stare at the crushed an broken petals on the rug. Start rootin round in the pouch Lireka gave me till I have a small handful of wilted petals in me hand.

'Wait, Iric. Look.' I hold the petals out fer him to see. Iric's eyes light up an he grabs the goblet an the kettle from the tray.

'How long does the cure take to work?'

'I dunno, it should stop the poison pretty quick, Aggy said, but it might be hours fore he wakes up.'

'That's all right.' Iric pours out a goblet of boilin water an I throw the petals in. 'As long as he can order the door open before the morning, we'll be all right.'

'Aggy won't.' I can barely speak past the hard lump in me throat. Marlow could be down there by now . . .

'Curse it all. You're right, Mold, I'm sorry. If only there were another way out of this room! What about the window?'

'We're three stories up,' I remind him, but he has put an idea in me head. 'The only way out of here is down, down there.' I point at the privy an Iric's face wrinkles in disgust. I shut off the flaps inside me nose an smile back.

'I'll send help as soon as I can.' Iric says, watchin me lift up the privy seat. His father's drunk the tonic now an he's sleepin peacefully fer the first time in days. The fever's gone, so's the wheezin, an he's even got a bit of colour in his cheeks. Those petals are a miracle cure, right enough. 'He's bound to wake up soon, then the guards will have to let me out and I'll come and find you, Mold. I promise.'

'I know.' I give him a quick smile an clamber on to the privy base.

'I can't thank you enough for what you've done, I'll do whatever I can to help you and Aggy. Anything.'

'It's all right Iric. I know ya will.'

I lower meself into the hole an start climbin down the ladder.

'Good luck!' Iric says fore replacin the privy seat. I keep climbin, lamp held firmly in me grasp. Back down to the sewer I swore I'd never use again.

It's easier now of course. Now I can shut out the stink but it don't change the fact it's still a sewer an I have to wade through . . . well, I don't wanna think about exactly what I'm wadin through.

I manage to find me way back to the small metal door Fergus pointed out when we were down here before an I wish he was here with me now, talkin me ear off like usual, but I slam the ache back down hard. I gotta focus on Aggy now an gettin to her fore that villain can hurt her.

The door to the dungeon is jammed shut but I barge it with me shoulder an it opens. I take a big swallow an walk through into the dingy, torchlit dungeon.

The dim corridor is cold an silent as the grave, I can feel the hairs pricklin down me neck. I speed up, the air comin out of me in white clouds as I gasp fer breath.

Her cell's empty, the door swings open but there's no sign of her anywhere. I spin round, check the other cells, maybe she's been moved, maybe she was—

'He come took her to the wet room.' The voice is a croak. I find the owner crouched in a corner of the cell opposite. He's wrapped entirely in rags with only a pair of eyes peerin out.

'What? Who took her?'

'Marlow.'

'What's the wet room? Where is it?'

'Down there.' A bony finger points down the corridor. 'Beware though, boy. No one disturbs him at work.'

'Work? What work?'

'Torture, boy. That's why the wet room has a drain in the middle. To wash away the blood.'

It feels like me head explodes. I remember how

Marlow cut the tongue from Ramsey's mouth an I run towards the room an crash through the door like a wild boar.

Aggy's hangin from the ceilin, a rope round her neck, an the scream rips from me stomach, hard an raw, echoin like a banshee's wail through the dungeon.

Chapter 25

The knife hits me in the shoulder. I fly backwards an crash into the doorway. Agony explodes in me head an everythin goes black fer a minute.

When I open me eyes again I'm bein dragged across the floor back into the wet room an the first thing I see is Aggy, limp as a rag doll. Horror crawls down me spine. I'm too late. After everythin I done. After the fire an the sewer an the Boggers. After losin Begsy an Fergus an nearly dyin I'm too damn late . . . again.

'She's not dead.' Marlow says, lockin the door behind him. 'She's merely fainted.'

I look more closely. I can just make out the gentle rise an fall of her chest an though she's got the rope round her throat her body's tied to a big metal pole in the floor, keepin the noose from crackin her neck.

'What did you do to her?' I let relief slip over me. If she aint dead yet then I can still save her.

'Oh, nothing much, not yet. I do like to take my time

with my victims. So . . .' He hunkers down next to me. 'Something's been bothering me and I need to know— exactly how did you get out?'

'What?' The blade's still embedded in me shoulder, burnin like a red-hot poker. It hurts to move, even breathe.

'Out of the fire. How did you escape? That hovel had no window and I barred the door. You should have burnt to a crisp.'

'There was a coal hole in the basement.' I decide to let him talk. While he's talkin I can think of a plan.

He lets out a dry laugh, sits back on his heels, an watches me writhe on the floor. 'You've got courage boy, I'll give you that. Shame about the brains though.'

'I escaped you three times,' I manage, though I can feel the blackness creepin in round the edges an the floor grows damp beneath me from the blood. 'I reckon that makes me cleverer an you!'

'Yes. You escaped, but then you ran straight back into trouble every time. Why you'd risk your young life for some old hag and a hovel in the slums is beyond me.'

'Course it is. You don't know nothin about love or loyalty,' I whisper.

'Love? I have no use for it. Hate is a much more useful emotion.'

'Fer someone like you. Someone who'd betray his country an his king.'

'This is not my country. I'm a mercenary, boy. Paid to fight, paid to protect Nash during the war. I was taken prisoner but Hexaba soon realized my worth and let me go. I've spent years working for Nash and his infernal intelligence network but at last my time has come. True power awaits me with the Boggers.'

'Yer plan aint gonna work. Godric's had the cure now spite everythin you done to stop it.'

'Enough! No more talking.'

He gets up, pulls a shinin silver blade from his boot.

'Bludengore will rip yer shrivelled heart out.'

'Shut up!' he hisses. 'There are no more chances for you, boy, and you should know that old crone you're so fond of will be next.' He looms towards me, the knife glints an slashes down towards me throat . . .

'Noooooo!' Aggy's scream echoes across the room. 'Stop, murderer!'

'Shut up you miserable old hag!' Marlow spins round an lunges in her direction an I use every bit of strength left to rip the knife from me shoulder an stagger to me feet. Gotta save Aggy . . .

'Oy! What's going on?' A fist pounds on the door.

'Help!' Aggy screams again. Marlow slaps her across the face.

'Open this door!' the voice shouts.

'I'm working,' Marlow bellows. 'Go away!'

There's noise an shoutin outside now. 'This is the Royal

Guard! We're coming in!' Godric must have woken, Iric had sent help just like he promised.

I can hear a key turnin in the lock, the door starts to open, Marlow leaps over to slam the door shut again but someone shoulders it open an sends Marlow flyin backwards. He crashes into me. Into the knife I'm holdin in me hand. His eyes bulge, blood leaks from his mouth.

I let go of the weapon an Marlow staggers backwards. I watch him slam into the wall, fall to his knees, an then lie still.

'Mold? Are you all right? Mold?' Aggy's voice seems to be comin from far away an she's gone all blurry round the edges. I feel dizzy.

I need to lie down. The floor is cold. Sticky with blood.

My blood.

Marlow's blood.

'Mold? Mold! Hold on!'

Floatin now.

Floatin . . .

Chapter 26

Aggy an me spend three days in the infirmary. I don't remember the first one much cos I was pretty out of it but when I wake up on day two Aggy's sittin next to me bed an holdin me hand. She's thinner an paler an there are shadows under her eyes but she's alive an she's here with me.

'Aggy?' Me voice sounds rough but she beams at me, her face lit up like a candle.

'Lawks a mercy, Mold, you had me worried.'

I cough. It jars me shoulder an makes me wince. Aggy offers me a cup of willow bark tea, sweetened with honey, an I take a few sips.

'You're one to talk,' I croak.

'But that louse near killed you, my love!'

He'd come pretty close true enough. There's a deep, throbbin ache in me shoulder an I feel weak as a newborn kitten.

'Is he dead?' I ask.

Aggy nods. 'He surely is, Mold, and that yellow-bellied

traitor Nash has gone missin. Iric's doin his best to run the place while his pa recovers.'

'He's all right then? Godric?'

'Yes, pet. That cure worked just like I said. Only it'll be a while fore he's on his feet again cos he was awful sick fer a while there.'

'An you?'

Aggy brushes the hair from me face. 'I'll be fine my love. Thanks to you.'

I smile at her. My Aggy, alive an whole an here with me.

'Yer a proper hero, Mold. Everyone says so.'

A big yawn cracks me jaw.

'You go back to sleep now, Mold. Rest, everything's fine. We're all fine thanks to you.'

'Not everyone.' Memories flood back. 'Not Begsy,' I whisper.

'I know.' Her eyes are filled with sorrow. 'Iric says they're gonna bury him in the royal crypt an there'll be a plaque on the wall, saying how brave he was and everything.'

'Not Fergus.'

'Fergus? That little lad who come to see me? Is he dead an all?'

I can't speak. Me throat hurts.

'Oh, I'm sorry, my lamb.' Aggy pulls me into her arms gentle as she can an holds me tight. 'It will be all right, pet.'

I close me eyes. It wasn't all right. Aggy was saved but the nightmare wasn't over. Not while Nash and the Bogger army were still out there.

Chapter 27

I'm half asleep when someone knocks at the door.

'Come in!' I yell from the fancy couch where I've spent the last few days.

Iric bursts into the room, his fair hair all sweaty an tousled like he's been runnin.

'Can you come now, Mold?'

'Come where?'

'To see my father. There's a big planning meeting later and I told him he needs to speak to you first.'

'I aint supposed to go out. Aggy'll kill me.'

'Just tell her I made you. You're living in the castle now so you have to do what I say. I'm the Prince aren't I?'

'Won't stop her tellin you off,' I mutter, shovin the blankets off of me.

'Where is she, anyway?'

'Down in the greenhouse with the other healers. They all think she's a marvel now she saved the King. I hardly see her any more.' I aint complainin though. Aggy's off the grog an happier an I've seen her in a long while.

I get to me feet an follow Iric down the hall an up some stairs. I have to stop an catch me breath at the top cos I'm still a bit weak but I'm better an I was anyway. Apart from missin Begsy an Fergus. That's an ache that never leaves me.

'This is it,' Iric says lookin surprisingly nervous. He pushes the door open an waves me in.

Godric is wrapped in a big woollen blanket an sittin at a huge oak table with a map of Pellegarno spread out in front of him. He's lookin much better an the last time I saw him but he's still thin an pale an Aggy reckons it'll be weeks fore he's back to full health.

'Father? This is Mold.'

Godric looks up an his dark-blue eyes survey me slowly.

'Mold. I hear I have much to thank you for.' He offers me his hand but I aint sure if I want to take it. Iric nudges me forward though an I don't suppose I've got much choice really.

I shake his hand slowly an try not to think about that hand signin all the Dai Kurlin away into slavery.

'I just wanted to confirm the information you have about the Boggers and their plans.'

'They were gonna attack once ye were dead. I reckon Nash escaped to the bogs an told em their plan failed but I dunno why they aint tried while you've been laid up.'

'Well, no doubt they fear my wrath now I am recovered. How big was their army exactly?'

'I saw about fifty soldiers.'

'Is that all?'

'Yes but they aint like normal Boggers!' I tell him. 'These are massive, huge, like monsters. They're dangerous Yer Majesty. I swear it.'

'Well, so am I, boy, so am I. As soon as I'm back on my feet I'll be destroying those beasts once and for all.'

'You mean destroyin the army, don't ye? Cos Lireka an the others aint done nothin, they saved yer life, didn't they?'

'I told him that, Mold,' Iric says.

'And I appreciate what they did,' Godric insists, 'but I'm not sure I can leave a potential enemy alive in my kingdom.'

'Your kingdom? This was their land first! Till you poxy Yellowhairs stole it!'

Godric's eyes bore into me. 'Iric, could you fetch me some more wine? My throat is terribly dry.'

'Of course, Father.' Iric gives me a quick grin fore he leaves but it don't help. I can feel me knees tremblin already.

'I am grateful for your help. Truly,' Godric says once the door's closed. 'But I want you to stop filling my son's head with nonsense.'

'Nonsense?'

'Yes. Nonsense! The Boggers are dangerous, I should

never have left a trace of them alive.' Hatred leaks from his every pore.

'You'd kill em all, wouldn't ye?' I whisper. 'Just like ye sold all of my people!'

'That was Nash!'

'You signed yer name on the order! You rewarded em for their help by sellin em into slavery.'

'And so what if I did?' he snaps back, his face red. 'I am the King! This is my land and the people are mine to do with as I wish!'

'A decent king looks after his people, not himself!'

'What would a Dregger brat like you know of ruling?'

'More an you I reckon!'

'You know nothing!' Godric yells, breakin off to cough an then settlin back in his chair. His voice is weary now. 'Do you think I wanted this life? Nothing but tedious meetings and boring paperwork and constant decisions? Nash was supposed to be the king, I had a very different life planned until the damn Boggers rose up and stole my wife from me!'

'Stole yer wife?'

'My Celeste! When she heard the news of how the Boggers had attacked Barlixtown and killed her family the shock sent her into early labour. Once the child was born she died in my arms and while her body was still warm I was forced to ride into battle and save my useless brother from his foolish mistakes.'

I can see now. How it had all got so out of hand. Godric blamed the Boggers fer the death of his wife. He always would.

'And when Father knew how Nash had failed, he made me king and I've been trapped ever since,' Godric tails off.

'Please, Yer Majesty, let the past go. Don't kill more innocents—'

'My wife was innocent! They killed her and I will kill them and I will not fail this time. As soon as I recover I will see the Boglands razed to the ground and every last Bogger DEAD!'

I back away. Away from the madness in his eyes, the rage in his soul, an the terrible, terrible smell of loneliness.

Iric is standin outside, a flask of wine in his hand. I can see from his face that he heard it all.

'Stars above, what do I do?' He looks at me, beggin me fer an answer so I give him one.

'You have to do what's right, Iric.'

'Yes. My father's not thinking straight, he's still ill I think.'

I let Iric believe that if he must but I can't let this happen. I won't. 'Then it's up to you to stop him makin a terrible mistake. Go to the swamps. Today. Talk to Lireka, maybe there's another way to end this apart from fightin? Maybe you can arrest Hexaba an Bludengore?'

'You think I should go against my father's orders?' Iric looks a bit pale at the thought.

'Those orders are wrong, Iric. If ye let it happen you'll regret it for ever.'

Iric straightens his shoulders. 'You're right, Mold. I need to take charge before it's too late. I'll try talking to them first, Mold, but I have to be prepared for fighting. If those Boggers attack we must be ready or innocent people will die.'

It wasn't perfect but at least it was a chance. 'All right then. That's fair I reckon.'

'I need to be able to find their village though.'

I swallow. Should I take him? Would I be betrayin the Skullensvar again or could I truly trust Iric? I breathe deep, let the scent of lemon fill me nostrils an it's all I need to make me decision.

'I'll take ye.'

'Are you sure, Mold? You're not really well enough are you?'

'I'm all right. I have to be. I can't let Lireka an the others die. We can't let another race be wiped out, Iric, we just can't.'

'We won't Mold. This plan will work, it has to.'

He rushes off to start organizin stuff an I slump down on the bed an wonder how the hell I'm gonna explain all this to Aggy.

Chapter 28

The good news is that by the time she's back she only has a few minutes or so to moan at me fore I have to leave with Iric an his guard.

'I aint letting you go, Mold!' She follows me down the stairs. 'It's too dangerous to go traipsing into the swamps an you aint even well yet.'

'I'm just gonna show Iric the way. I won't have to do much.'

'But you're only a lad, they shouldn't make ye do it.'

I step outside into the courtyard where Iric an his men are mountin up. 'They aint makin me. I'm goin cos it's the right thing to do.' It is, I know it. 'I might be able to stop a war, Aggy, an save lives an that's important, aint it?'

'Lordy, Mold, when did you get so big and brave?'

I smile at her an give her another hug, drinkin in a lungful of the deep, lilac scent that is the very heart of her an no longer masked by the stink of gin on her breath. 'We'll be together soon I promise. Iric says he's gonna find you a shop, here in the city.'

'Well,' she sniffs an wipes her face. 'You just make sure you come home in one piece. I can't keep fixing you up!'

I kiss Aggy's soft cheek. 'I'll come back, Aggy, I promise.'

It takes ten minutes more fore we finally manage to leave Aggy an her warnins behind. I hold tight to Iric's waist while he steers his great stallion down the paved road towards the docks.

⁂

Catchin sight of the mist-covered river again makes me guts clench an I have to breathe slow to stop meself pukin all over Iric's back. I can do this. I can.

Iric ties up his horse an helps me down. 'Just wait here, Mold, I need to talk to the men and get things organized, all right?' I nod an watch him walk off to join the two hundred men marchin onto the dockside. I stroke Iric's nut-brown stallion Valiant an try to stay calm.

'It'll be fine,' I whisper to the horse. 'Just lead em to the camp, that's all I have to do.'

Valiant whickers at me an I let him lick me palm an the sweat that covers it. If Fergus could take on Bludengore all alone then I can be brave enough to face him with two hundred soldiers beside me. He might be tough but he aint invincible, is he?

Sommink in the air drags me away from me worryin an back to the dock. I open me nostrils wide an drink in the scent. It takes me a second to recognize it but then I'm sure.

Chapter 29

Nash.

I can smell him. The rottin stench of dead rats aint hidden any more, but where is he? I follow me nose to the opposite bank an there, in the mist, is a raft.

Standin on top of it is Nash.

'Iric!' I shout. 'Iric, look!'

Slowly, people turn an when they see the betrayer floatin towards us silence falls over the dock. As he gets closer there are gasps from the crowd. His clothes are filthy an ragged, his shoulders slumped, an there's a red-raw gash across his brow. I wonder if the Boggers weren't quite as happy to see him as he thought they'd be?

'Iric!' he shouts when he sees us watchin. 'Dear nephew, can you ever forgive me? I have been such a fool.' His voice breaks with a sob.

'You have committed a great crime against my father, against us all,' Iric says but I can see his anger drainin away already.

'I know, I was mad with jealousy. Is . . . is Godric recovered?'

'Not quite.'

'But he will live?'

'No thanks to you.'

Nash steps off the raft an falls to his knees, his shoulders shakin. 'I can only thank heaven that my plan failed, that my dear brother survived. I can only beg you to give me another chance.'

I can't stop a little worm of suspicion creepin into me mind. He's always been a good actor, I just wish I could be sure of his intentions. An then I realize, maybe this time I can be. I open up me nostril flaps an breathe in deep.

'Please, Iric? We are family after all?' He holds his arms out. Iric steps forward, towards his uncle, towards the river.

'I am so glad you've had a change of heart, Uncle.'

'You need never doubt me again, I swear it.' *Me nostrils prickle with the sweet tang of manure, of lies . . .*

'Iric, stop! Don't!' I bellow, runnin after him even though I'll never reach him in time. 'It's a trap!'

Iric hears me, he turns his head.

Nash's dagger flies past his ear stead of goin through his eye.

Iric stumbles back away from the river to the sound of Nash's laughter.

'Don't go dear nephew! Stay. The fun's only just started, I have some friends I want you to meet.' At his words a mass of giant Boggers erupt from the water behind him, their great bodies drippin wet an covered in weed.

Bludengore's furious snarl sets off the others an their growlin fills the air like a pack of hungry wolves in winter. The scent of fear fills me nostrils as the guards get a good look at their enemy fer the first time. These aint the small an scrawny Boggers they've seen before. These are terrifyin monsters big enough to scare anyone.

'We are not family, not any more,' Iric spits through gritted teeth. His bodyguards have rushed forward to protect him an Alnor leads Valiant down to the dock so Iric can mount.

'Fine,' Nash snaps. 'Surrender the crown to me now or I will unleash my army and take it from you by force!'

I sneak through the guards an grab Iric's ankle as he shoves his foot into the stirrup. 'You aint got enough men to fight all them. There's more an double the number I thought!'

'I know but I have to try. I have to stop them here, if they reach the city there'll be a slaughter.'

'But . . .'

Iric claps his hand on me shoulder. 'I've sent word to the garrison for help, Mold. Until they get here I will protect the people, it's my job.' I nod. Iric settles himself on Valiant's back. 'Now you need to get away from here, go home, back to Aggy.'

'Ye want me to leave ye, after gettin ye into this mess?'

'If it wasn't for you we wouldn't even be here to fight and they'd already be attacking the city! If it wasn't for you I'd already be dead. You've done enough Mold, we're all in your debt. Now it's my turn.' He turns his focus to Nash who's standin on his raft again an dwarfed by the monstrous army that surrounds him. I step back but I can't get too far as the soldiers are all pressin forward.

'This is your last chance, Iric!' Nash shouts.

'We will never surrender. Rather you end up ruler of a graveyard then give in to your threats!'

'Be it on your head then, boy,' Nash mutters an turns to survey his great army. 'Attack!' he yells.

The guards brace emselves but nothin happens. The Boggers remain still as statues. 'Attack, now!' he shouts more loudly but they seem not to even hear him.

A small titter starts among the guards.

Nash's face blooms red as a tomato an he glares at Bludengore.

'I'm telling them to attack! Why won't they attack?' he hisses at Bludengore.

'This army is mine,' Bludengore's deep voice rumbles from his huge chest. 'It follows my command.'

'And you swore an oath to follow mine!' Nash snaps. 'So do as you're told.'

The giant Bogger moves so fast I almost miss it but the next second he has Nash in his grasp, that huge hand circlin his throat, sword tip aimed at his heart.

'No one orders Bludengore! I am Prince of the Skullensvar and oaths made to betrayers like you mean nothing.' He thrusts his blade into Nash's chest. 'I will wear the crown little man, not you.'

He yanks his blood-soaked sword out an lets Nash's lifeless body sink below the surface. His arm rises into the sky an he lets loose a terrible war cry that scares the birds from the trees an turns me knees to water. His army echoes him an as one they surge to shore, blades aloft, crashin into the waitin guards like a tidal wave.

Chapter 30

I hide under the dock, the sounds of battle ragin all around me. Swords clashin, men screamin, horses dyin, an the river where I'm standin waist-deep is stained red with their blood.

I'm frozen in place, eyes tight shut, hands over me ears, tremblin like a leaf in a storm. 'Be brave,' I whisper to meself, over an over like a prayer, but it does no good. The first few minutes of fightin had been worse than anythin I could imagine. Blood an fear an hate an death mixed together in a boilin stench that near knocked me over till I remembered how to close me nostrils. It was too late by then though. Me escape route was blocked an I had no choice but to hide.

A splash nearby forces me to look behind. The huge, bloated corpse of a Bogger floats towards me, great bloody wounds across its chest. The current pushes it closer an closer an I can't seem to tear me eyes away from the gore-stained body spite the sickness risin in me throat. I stay locked in place while it slowly drifts past but just when I think it's gone, cold fingers grip me wrist an tug me off me feet an out of the shelterin platform.

Chokin on river water I struggle an fight like a wild cat but the Bogger only pulls me closer till I'm lookin straight into its snarlin face. Terror shoots through me an I kick out, stompin on his wounded stomach an then jabbin me fingers into his eyes.

Soon as he lets me go I paddle away fast as I can an end up crashin into the raft Nash was usin. I drag meself onto the wooden boards an collapse in a shiverin heap fer a few minutes.

I manage to lift me head after a bit an stare in horror at the vicious battle on the shore an the scores of dead bodies litterin the ground. It looks like the guards are puttin up a good fight but the Boggers are pushin em hard. Their army's somehow doubled in size in just a week an now it's smashin its way through the guards like a batterin ram with Bludengore at the front roarin like a bull an sweepin soldiers aside with his great club.

I can see Iric fightin in the centre, wieldin his sword like he was born to it. His mount Valiant kicks out with his front hooves, takin down Bogger after Bogger. Alnor an his personal guard surround him, fightin as best they can, but I can see em strugglin against the sheer strength of the monster army.

'Keep fighting!' Iric shouts, his sword whirlin. 'We are men of Westenburg!'

The guards rally for their prince an arrows start flyin down from the castle longbows, piercin the thick hides of the Boggers, an I can see a platoon of fresh guards come into view. Reinforcements from the city barracks. They march towards the battle, an even when they see the monsters waitin below they keep walkin, spears at the ready. I know they'll keep fightin to the last man but I'm scared they're gonna lose, that those monsters will take the city an Aggy an everyone in it'll be killed.

A dead Bogger knocks into me raft an I watch it float up the river. I open me nose flaps the smallest amount, just to see if I can cope, an the faint whiff of fresh blood an rotten eggs makes me nose twitch cos I've smelt that mix before, in Hexaba's hut. I take a deeper breath an this time the rich metallic stench of the blood fungus she'd sent me lookin fer wafts into me nostrils, an Lireka's warnin about the dangerous magic she'd use em fer is poundin in me head . . .

Chapter 31

I start paddlin down the river, followin the bloody scent, a terrible fear buildin in me mind that Hexaba had sommink to do with these new monsters an she was usin the mushrooms I found.

The smell gets stronger, it makes me guts clench but I keep goin till I see a big muddy area where the swamp's been churned up by giant feet an I get as close as I can fore tyin up the raft an settin off on foot along the bank.

I'm gettin closer, the smell's near chokin me but there's sommink else there, underneath . . . I open me nostril flaps wide as I can an the stink of the privies rushes in. Fergus? It can't be!

Not unless it's his dead body . . .

Me belly heaves. I chuck up. Over an over till nothin but green bile comes out, tears an snot are coverin me face—

'Mold?'

I spin round.

It's Fergus. An he aint dead. He's standin there covered

in mud with leaves in his hair an he's grinnin at me large as life.

Me knees wobble. 'How . . . I mean . . . what . . . I mean . . . Bludengore killed ye, didn't he?'

'It was yer friend Lireka who saved me.' He pulls up his shirt an shows me the vicious claw marks cuttin through his rib cage. Like the scar on me leg they'd healed to a thick red line but I could see they'd near sliced him in two. 'She found me an looked after me fer days in an old hut over there while I was sick with the fever.'

'Stars above, I thought ye were dead, ye smelly little tyke!' I grab him an hug him an try not to cry. I press me face against the top of his head an breathe him in but instead of sewers all I'm smellin is grass, fresh cut grass, an I know that sweetness is the heart of him. Always has been.

Part of me wants to pick him up an run. Leave the swamps an never come back but I can't. Not yet.

'Where's Lireka now?' I ask.

'She had to go. There was a fight or something in the village yesterday. We heard screams and everything. Lireka said they were stealing the eggs and she left to go help. What's going on, Mold?'

'I aint sure exactly but I don't reckon it's good. Come on.' I fill him in on what's been happenin with Iric an Nash an Bludengore as we creep further along the bank.

The stench explodes at the edge of a black bog an Fergus an I hide behind the prickly bushes that surround it, our faces peerin through the leaves at the weird contents of the mud.

Great grey boulders rise out of the steamin ooze an seem to throb an pulse as if they're alive. Hexaba has her cauldron set up on the edge, outside of a tumbledown shack, an she stirs the noxious mixture fore goin inside. She comes back out with an egg, about the same size as the one I saw in the nestin bogs. There's a hole already drilled in the top of the shell an she drips a ladle of her potion into the egg fore plantin it deep into the mud.

The egg starts to swell an grow before our eyes, near doublin in size in just a few minutes.

'What's she doin, Mold?' Fergus whispers.

'She's makin monsters. That's what they've been doin while we were waitin for em to attack.' I can hardly believe it but she is. There must be a hundred or more eggs still in the bog. Most of em twice my size. If they hatch an all . . .

'We've gotta stop her,' Fergus says.

'I know.' I think fer a minute. 'Next time she goes in that shack you go over there an tie the door shut with some vine. I'll destroy the eggs fore more of those monsters can hatch.'

Fergus nods an soon as she's inside again he sneaks down to the shack. I wait till he's got the door good an tied fore followin him. I pick up an old shovel lyin on the banks an move over to the first boulder-like egg. I raise the shovel in the air an bring the sharp end down on the shell. A crack rips across the top an yellow-stained liquid starts leakin through, along with the pong of rotten fish.

Another hard smack an the shell shatters.

'Nooooo!' Hexaba's wail comes from the shack but the door stays firmly tied spite her strugglin.

I smash through the second shell. And the third. Hexaba's wailin grows louder.

I keep goin, teeth gritted, smashin as many as I can till the cabin door finally gives way with a screech an Hexaba bursts out, her face a snarlin mask of rage.

'Nooooo! What have you done?'

'I won't let ye kill everyone ye mad old witch!'

'They deserve it! After what they did to us they all deserve to die.' She marches through the swamp towards me.

'An so you steal yer own people's eggs an turn em into monsters? How is that helpin yer people?'

'They must make sacrifices if we are to have victory! I have slaved for years trying to recreate the potion that made Bludengore. Now that I have, no one will stop us!'

She launches herself at me an knocks us both into the mud. Her wiry fingers find me throat an start squeezin, but Fergus throws himself at her with all he's got.

She lashes out at him with a clawed fist, knocks him sprawlin in the swamp an stares at us with hate-filled eyes. She starts chantin some strange words I've never heard before.

Crackin sounds float across the air along with the whiff of fish as all the eggs I hadn't smashed yet start to hatch. Hexaba's words are givin em life an they're risin up, eyes wide open, howlin like starvin wolves.

Hexaba shrieks with laughter as the monsters unfold from their eggs, stretchin up almost twice the size of a man.

'Can you see the end of the Yellowhair now, boy? With my new army we will rule Pellegarno again. She lifts her hand an points at one of the Boggers. 'They are mine, they do my bidding. Bludengore was made with the blood of his father but I used my own blood to help these ones grow, they are part of me now, we are linked.' The Bogger moves all stiff and unsteady on his feet like an picks Fergus up from the ground.

'I could have the boy ripped apart if I choose . . .'

'No! Leave him be!' I yell, sick at the sight of Fergus in the clutches of that monster. I rush at the Bogger, tryin to knock him over, but his arm flies out an sends me whooshin through the air. I smash down in the mud, every bone in me body jarred an bruised.

'You cannot defeat my beautiful children, stupid boy! They're too strong, too powerful. The blood fungus you found has made it so!'

She's right of course. I've no chance against one of

them but what she said earlier finally sinks into me brain. If they were linked to Hexaba that made her the weak point, the only way to stop em was to stop her. I squirm forward, me fingers reach out fer the spade handle . . .

'He will die, they will all die!' Hexaba cackles wildly as she rushes towards me. I make a desperate lunge fer the handle an smash the spade into Hexaba's body, she spins an falls face-first into the mud.

That same second Fergus pokes his fingers into the Bogger's eyes an it stumbles backwards blindly an brings its giant foot down onto Hexaba's head, squelchin it deep into the black bog. I hear her gurgle, watch her hands an feet scrabble in the mud wildly fer a few seconds fore they slow, become still.

A few small bubbles appear on the surface an then stop.

I reckon she's dead.

As if in answer the giant monsters collapse in heaps all across the swamp, almost like someone reached in their heads an turned em off.

I drop the spade an squelch over to Fergus, who's been dropped on his head an looks a mite dazed. He sits up an rubs his face.

'What's goin on? What happened?'

I slump down next to him. 'She's dead,' I tell him. 'An so's her ruddy army.'

'Thank the stars fer that,' Fergus says. 'I'm flamin well worn out.'

Chapter 32

Me an Fergus manage to stumble back to the raft but everythin hurts, even me hair. All I can think about is gettin back, back to Aggy, back to a life without runnin an fightin an death. The stench of it lingers like day-old kippers an I'll be glad to be rid of it.

'D'you reckon them other Boggers fightin Iric have died an all, Mold?' Fergus asks, climbin on board.

'I hope so.' I push the raft into the stream an jump on. 'I hope that's a flamin end to the whole thing an life'll get back to normal at last.'

'Yeah.' Fergus sniffs. 'You wanna get back to Aggy and yer old life I expect.'

'I don't think I can go back to the Dregs. Not without Begsy there . . . but Iric said he's gonna see about gettin us a shop an a new house in the city, to thank us like fer what we done.'

I watch Fergus' shoulders slump further an further as he listens.

'That's nice.' He rubs his face with his ragged sleeve an I decide to put him out of his misery.

'Yep, it's gonna be great. Just me, Aggy . . . an you if ye like?'

His head spins round an he stares at me, mouth hangin open.

'Mmm . . . me?'

'Yeah. I reckon Aggy wouldn't mind another chick fer her nest.'

'Really?'

'Aye. There's one condition though.' I make me face serious as I can an Fergus gulps.

'What? I'll do anything, Mold. Anything.'

'Well . . .' I pause long as I can. 'You have to have a bath first AND use some ruddy soap!'

I splash him with me paddle an he grins.

I aint grinnin fer long though cos paddlin back up that river is a proper slog I tell ya. It don't help when dead Boggers start driftin past, their huge bodies limp an lifeless.

I get a twinge of guilt knowin it was me that ended their short lives cos it weren't their fault was it? They got made into monsters with no choice about nothin.

In the end I have to close me nostril flaps to shut out the smell an just keep on paddlin. Get back to Aggy. Even if she orders me on the sofa fer a month I won't mind. Nothin sounds better an sleepin right now.

'D'you reckon they're gonna give us medals?' Fergus asks.

'Oh aye, five of em probably,' I tell him.

'Really?'

'No!'

'We should get medals though after what we done,' Fergus mutters. 'I mean we saved the King, uncovered the poison plot, got rid of Marlow, and Nash, and Hexaba, and her whole flaming army!'

'Aye, we're proper heroes aint we? The privy pipe cleaner an the Dregger.'

'You are a hero, Mold. No doubt about that.'

Funny thing is, as I'm forcin me way through the mass of dead Boggers that clog the river near the docks, I don't feel much like a hero at all.

Chapter 33

The battleground is empty. There's no sign of any live Boggers an most of the Westenburg soldiers are marchin back up towards the city, many of em nursing wounds or supportin their injured mates. There are a few guards spread out on the banks draggin out the dead, an if I squint I can see carts headin up the hill to the city loaded down with bodies.

So many lives lost. An what fer? Revenge? Power? Hatred? I was so tired of it all.

'Is that the Prince?' Fergus points up at the dock an I see Iric, battered an bloodstained but unhurt, givin out orders, an I paddle over an drop the anchor.

Alnor sees us an helps us up onto the wooden platform.

'Mold!' Iric beams when he sees me. 'I was so worried about you. Where have you been?'

'I—'

'He was with me in the swamps,' Fergus blurts out, in his excitement. 'We broke all the eggs to stop that

Hexaba from makin even more monsters an there was a big fight cos she was real mad at us an she got her head squished in the mud an then all her army died.'

Iric's mouth gapes a bit then he blinks an looks at me.

'This is Fergus,' I explain.

'Oh, I wondered what happened. The battle wasn't going well, I thought we were going to lose and then all of a sudden, their army started to fall. Just collapsed like rag dolls.'

'Mold done it,' Fergus says. 'But I helped a bit.'

'Then you have saved us. All of us.' Iric slaps Fergus on the back an he puffs out his chest like a turkey.

I feel queasy though. Even with me nostril flaps tight closed I can't escape the stench of death. It's in me head an all around me.

'Cor look at that,' Fergus breathes, his finger pointin over at the opposite bank. We turn an see Skullensvar slowly emergin from the trees. Looks like the whole rag-tag tribe have come from the bogs, maybe a couple of hundred altogether, men, women, an kids.

The women catch sight of the dead bodies floatin in the river an their cries rip through the still air, silencin us all. We watch em plunge into the shallows an cry over their lost children.

I can see Fergus's bottom lip tremblin an I feel like cryin meself. It's all so sad.

Iric coughs. 'Fergus, I wonder if you'd do me a favour?'

'Me?' Fergus's eyes go wide.

'Yes, I need someone to take my horse Valiant up to his stables and make sure he's fed and brushed.'

'I'll do it! I love horses!'

'Excellent.' Iric smiles at him. 'You can ride him with Alnor leading if you like?'

Fergus all but pulls Alnor's arm off, he's draggin him so fast up the road towards Valiant.

'Was it true what he said about the eggs?' Iric asks me when he's gone.

'Aye.' I explain in a bit more detail.

'What a waste.' He stares over at the grievin Skullensvar, his face shadowed with sadness. 'That's enough now. Enough. My father will listen to me this time, I promise you. I will find a way to make peace between our people, and if he can't accept it and do what's best for Pellegarno, then he'll have to leave. We can't carry on this way.'

Iric straightens his shoulders an starts walkin up the dock towards the castle. I can see the battle has hardened him, but in a good way I reckon. Like molten steel tempered in freezin water.

I'm runnin to catch him up when the whole platform trembles. Once . . . twice . . . Iric an I are frozen in place when up ahead the wooden planks explode into the air an a great green monster bursts up from below.

Bludengore.

He's injured, one of his huge arms hangs uselessly from the shoulder an his face is badly mangled. He should be weaker but if anythin he just looks more dangerous an ever.

But why aint he dead like the others? Me mind races till it remembers Hexaba's words. She'd used her mate's blood to make him, not her own. Hexaba's death had no effect on him. Well, I swallow hard, cept fer rilin him up that is.

'Prince.' He spits the word out. 'The time has come for you to answer for the crimes of your kind.' He moves closer, the sword in his good hand pointin straight at Iric. 'We will fight now, you and I, prince versus prince, one on one. Unless you are a spineless coward like your father?'

Iric grits his teeth, draws his sword, an prepares fer battle. He'll lose. He must know it. Without his horse an his armour an his guards Iric won't stand a chance. But he won't back down neither.

Bludengore moves in hard an fast, their swords screech as they meet once, twice, three times, an already I can see Iric's arm tremble under the weight of those blows.

He does his best. I watch him defend over an over but Bludengore gives him no rest, no chance to break free, an a few minutes in he draws blood. A deep gash right across Iric's cheek.

The Skullensvar Prince pauses to grin an then attacks again with renewed fire. Poundin Iric over an over, each time findin a weak spot an openin up a wound.

It feels like hours but it's only been minutes. I'm frozen in place, watchin Iric suffer. He's sweat-soaked, weakened from blood loss, an fadin fast but he finds the strength fer one more move, rolls under his opponent's guard an thrusts his sword up into Bludengore's stomach.

Bludengore bellows an backhands Iric hard with his fist, yankin Iric's sword out of his hand an throwin it into the river with a grunt.

It's over. Up an down the river I can see guards rushin to help but they're too far away. I watch Bludengore limp over to his victim, ready to strike the final blow. Bludengore lifts his sword . . .

'Wait! It was me, me who destroyed your army!' I shout an he pauses long enough fer me to rush over to Iric an kneel by his side.

Bludengore snarls. 'You Dai Kurlin scum do nothing but betray us. You can die with your precious prince.'

'It aint me betrayin yer tribe though, it's you!' I shout, loud as I can, hopin me voice might carry across the river. 'You an yer ma sacrificed a whole generation of Skullensvar fer revenge, the future of yer tribe is floatin dead in the river instead of growin up to be healthy young Skullensvar.'

A low growlin comes from Bludengore's chest an I can feel meself shakin under that vicious glare. I keep talkin though. Might as well. I aint got long left an I need to get the truth out.

'You may kill me an Iric but the guards are already comin, ye can't kill em all. You'll die today an then what do ye think Godric'll do in revenge? He'll soak the bogs in oil an burn it down, killin every last Skullensvar in Pellegarno!' I take a breath, Iric's hand sneaks into mine an squeezes, givin me the last burst of courage I need. 'If ye really love yer tribe an yer people then ye'll let Iric live an forge a peace where yer tribe can thrive. You'll let the future win an not the past!'

I stop talkin. Bludengore moves closer an I grip Iric's hand tight enough to hurt.

'I have sworn an oath to avenge my people...' Bludengore pauses an a little bit of hope squirms in. Maybe he's listened to me. Maybe he'll do the right thing... 'And avenge them I will!'

Madness flares across his ghastly face an his sword sweeps down towards our heads. I squeeze me eyes tight shut.

There's movement over me head, whisperin past, not a sword, more like tiny birds... an carried on em the noxious scent of poison. Every deadly poison from the swamp; the purple Narlo frog, the stripy Delen snake an the scarlet coral fish...

I hear Iric gasp an open me eyes to see Bludengore, his mouth gapin with shock, his massive chest peppered with tiny, feathered, poisoned darts.

The sword falls from his fingers an he crashes to his

knees as the toxins rush through his system. A moment later his heart stops entirely an his body thuds to the floor.

I spin me head round an see the Skullensvar on the opposite bank, blowpipes in their hands. They had listened to me an they had taken the future into their own hands.

Chapter 34

I aint sure exactly what Iric said to his pa but Godric left soon after. Gone on one of his ships to live the life he'd always wanted, so I hear, an leavin his son to try an heal Pellegarno.

Iric's busier an ever now that he's king but he don't mind all the work an he still finds time to come an visit me every week.

True to his word he'd found us a cosy little shop in town where Aggy could sell her potions an cures an there was plenty of room out back fer us all to live.

I keep me eye out fer him an I when I see him comin I duck out the back door with me bag an a list of ingredients, leavin Aggy an Fergus to deal with the crowds of customers. Those two are happy as pigs in muck mixin an choppin from dawn till dusk, but I don't much like bein cooped up so I go out every day foragin fer all the things they need.

'What important stuff you been up to today then?'

I ask as we head up the road. I can't quite get used to him bein the King but he aint changed much really.

'Actually I was at a council meeting all morning and it went really well.' I can tell that already from the bounce in his step. 'Lireka's invited us all to go to her village for dinner next week and Meg wants us to visit the Dregs next month and sample her amazing pies. Everyone has plans for change and everyone is actually working together at last.'

'Blimey.' Iric had got a lot of stick fer settin up a council to co-rule with him, specially a council made up of Skullensvar an Dreggers an merchants stead of just toffs but it was workin an I was right proud of him.

'And what important stuff have you been up to?' Iric asks.

I snort an set me bag down near the mill stream so I can cut rushes from the banks. 'Well, I found Ma Connor's cat Snuffkins locked in the coal bunker an she gave me a toffee.'

I was hopin fer a laugh but Iric barely manages a smile. 'Are you sure you're happy, Mold?' he asks.

'Course I'm happy.' I wade deeper into the stream, dig out the wild garlic growin on the opposite bank.

'But is this what you really want? To dig up plants an mushrooms all day and find people's lost cats? You could go travelling, see the world.'

'I've got all I want right here. Aggy an Fergus safe an sound, a warm house to live in, an a decent job. I've done enough travellin thank ye very much.'

'Is it because you don't want to leave Aggy and Fergus?' Iric asks me.

'No. I just wanna stay here, where I belong.'

He smiles then an changes the subject. Perhaps he knows why I'm stayin. He'd shown me the letters he'd sent out to all the Isles, offerin a home to any Dai Kurlin who wanted to return an a reward fer their owners. I'm sure someone'll take him up on it, I'm sure one day they'll come home.

When he's gone I take a wander down to the docks an I look down the river towards Shillin. I watch the barges arrivin an I wonder if today just might be that day.

Pellegarno's natural world

Name	Description	Habitat	Uses	Danger rating 1-10
Blood Fungus	A dark red, squashy, wide, flat mushroom with a strong iron smell.	Grows deep in the mud of the swamps, very hard to find, and highly sought after by potion makers.	Will increase the power of potions exponentially.	9
Camberlinan Orchid	A tall flower with rows of lilac blooms along its green stem and long orange leaves. Honey-like smell.	Very rare. Single flowers grow only in the thick mud of the bogs.	Can cure almost any poison if you steep the leaves in boiling water and drink.	0
Dogweed	A pernicious fast-growing weed, with flat yellow leaves and white seedpods that explode and spread seeds far and wide. Smells like rotten limes.	Can grow almost anywhere. Found in the bogs, and in fields and farms.	The juice from steeping the leaves in boiling water is a poison.	7
Gurdiskar Root	The root portion of the flowering gurdiskar plant is dark black and shiny, about the size of a fist. Harsh, acrid smell.	Prefers to grow in forests, under shade. Now found only rarely in Pellegarno and highly prized.	Pounding the root will release juices that are tasteless and highly poisonous.	10
Henbane	A medium-sized green plant with white flowers. Cloying, sweet odour.	Grows wild in most environments. Hardy and prolific.	Seeds, root and leaves are all poisonous, can cause visions and a deathly sleep.	9

Julanti plants	A tall green plant with wide pink flowers and a strong scent. It defends itself from predators by spitting out a harsh acid from its core.	Grows at the base of fig trees. Mainly found in the bogs of Pellegarno.	Dried and powdered, the leaves are used to treat diarrhoea.	6.5
Mangrove	Small leafy shrubs and trees. In the mud, their roots keep the swamps stable and provide a firm base to walk on.	The bogs have vast numbers of mangroves.	They provide homes for many birds, animals, and insects. Fish and snakes also find homes around the root system. The Skullensvar make use of them for shelter.	0
Strangler Vines	Tall dark green vines that sense vibration and snatch up their prey, strangle it and then dissolve it slowly inside their root bulb.	In dark parts of the bog, away from sunlight.	The vines can be eaten raw and provide a good, sweet energy source.	8
Swamp Thistles	Spiky dark green weed with a bristly head that will cause a painful rash if touched.	This water plant sinks its roots deep into the mud of the bogs.	Good for treating warts.	3
Verlinx	A small brown, thorn-filled bush with red berries every summer. The thorns are long and cause a painful sensation when embedded in skin.	Grows on the edge of the bog where the sun is strong.	Small birds nest in these bushes, using their natural protection to stay safe from the thorns and the berries as a food source.	2
Delen Snake	A thin vicious viper with brown and yellow stripes. Attacks at any provocation unleashing a massive amount of toxin in one bite.	Likes a small hole to use as a den, preferably somewhere dark and swampy. Can move on land or in water.	The flesh can be eaten. The skin and fangs are used for tribal decorations. The venom can be extracted and used for arrows and blow darts.	10

Murklizard	A long moss-coloured reptile, about seven to ten feet in length. It lurks in the mud and drowns its prey by pulling it under before eating it.	Found in the bogs, often impossible to spot beneath the mud.	Their skin is excellent for wearing once tanned like leather. Their flesh is good to eat. Their bones are powdered and used for strengthening tonics.	8
Purple Narlo Frog	A small dark purple frog, which leaches a poison through its skin to protect it from being eaten by birds.	Needs damp, humid conditions. Mainly lives on the mangrove trees in the bog.	The frogs are trapped by the Skullensvar and the poison leeched from their skins. Once heated it becomes non toxic and excellent for the topical numbing of pain.	9
Scarlet Coral Fish	A beautiful fish, with many fins and a long tail. Any pressure on the fins will release barbs which inject a fatal dose of poison.	Likes small, dark, cool pools to live in, often found in the bogs.	The fish is prized for its colour. If caught and boiled the liquid can be used as a red dye. The poison is used on arrows and blow darts. It paralyses the victim and then dissolves the insides.	10
Yurg	A dark brown slimy slug-like creature, has strong suckers on its underside. It releases ravenous grubs which devour everything in their path before returning to their host. The Yurg then absorbs their poo for sustenance.	Found in dark, damp places. It is very fond of the sewer system in Westenburg	No practical use has been found as yet.	1

Yurg 'Gobble' Grubs	Small black beetle-like insects with very sharp teeth that can devour flesh and bone. Have a voracious appetite and will eat anything.	Live inside the Yurg except when released to feed.	No practical use has been found as yet.	8
Dai Kurlin (sniffler)	This unusual species of human has a slight build and average height with dark skin and hair. They have developed extremely large noses with unique flaps inside which enable them to control their remarkable sense of smell.	Native to Pellegarno, they live in tribes and hunt in the open plains and forests of Northern Pellegarno.	Their noses allow them to hunt the prey they require and forage the land with huge success. They are also able to smell the emotions of others and use this ability to live in harmony with each other and their neighbours.	7.5
Skullensvar (bogger)	This species of mammal is human like in shape with a small and wiry build. They have green scales over their bodies, webbed feet, and black claws.	Native to Pellegarno they live in close knit tribes exclusively in the southern boglands.	Great swimmers and climbers they hunt and forage the swamps with ease and protect their homes with ferocious loyalty.	8
Skullensvar-warrior	Giant modified boggers, eight feet tall, armour-like scales, black claws, and sharp teeth. Created by Hexaba using Skullensvar eggs and a potion including her own blood.	Found in the bogs.	Excellent, extremely strong soldiers, they worship their creator, Hexeba, and follow her son, Bludengore, the first warrior, Prince of the Skullensvar and mightiest of them all	9

Acknowledgements

My first thank you goes to Jude Hutchinson for being a true Kindred Spirit over the years.

Thanks also to everyone from the 'Crit Group of No Name' Karen, Larissa, Paula, Michelle, Tania, Allison, Meira, Peter, Gail, and especially my amazing chum Miriam Craig for all their support over the years.

Enormous gratitude goes to my wonderful GEA mentors Maurice Lyon and Imogen Cooper.

Huge thanks to all the fab bookish people I've met along the way through SCBWI, GEA, and Twitter but most especially the lovely Jennifer Killick and the fabulous Patience Pants Brigade—James Nicol and Vashti Hardy without whom I'd no doubt be a gibbering mess by now!

Many grateful thanks to my passionate, committed, and truly lovely agent Kate Shaw and to my publishers at OUP where Liz Cross, Clare Whitson, Elv Moody, and a whole team have nurtured me with such kindness.

I really can't thank my husband Steve enough for being so wonderful throughout this journey, supporting me and my dreams with endless patience.

Finally then, a ginormous thank you to my son Luke who is the reason I started writing again, the inspiration behind this book, and my best and biggest supporter throughout.